GUNK

By the same author

SEND NUDES

SABA SAMS

GUNK

BLOOMSBURY CIRCUS
LONDON · OXFORD · NEW YORK · NEW DELHI · SYDNEY

BLOOMSBURY CIRCUS
Bloomsbury Publishing Plc
50 Bedford Square, London, WC1B 3DP, UK
Bloomsbury Publishing Ireland Limited,
29 Earlsfort Terrace, Dublin 2, D02 AY28, Ireland

BLOOMSBURY, BLOOMSBURY CIRCUS and the Circus logo are trademarks of
Bloomsbury Publishing Plc

First published in Great Britain 2025

A catalogue record for this book is available from the British Library

ISBN: HB: 978-1-5266-2180-1; TPB: 978-1-5266-6648-2;
EBOOK: 978-1-5266-2181-8; EPDF: 978-1-5266-8820-0;
WATERSTONES EDITION: 978-1-5266-9398-3

2 4 6 8 10 9 7 5 3 1

Typeset by Integra Software Services Pvt. Ltd.
Printed and bound in Great Britain by Clays Ltd, Elcograf S.p.A

MIX
Paper | Supporting
responsible forestry
FSC® C018072

To find out more about our authors and books visit www.bloomsbury.com
and sign up for our newsletters.

For product safety related questions contact productsafety@bloomsbury.com

For my mother, who I used to wish would stop
swearing and smoking in public; who has stayed
boldly herself, from the very beginning,
so that I might do the same.

To create a being out of oneself is very serious. I am creating myself. And walking in complete darkness in search of ourselves is what we do. It hurts. But these are the pains of childbirth: a thing is born that is.

— Clarice Lispector, *Água Viva*

How's one going to get through it all? How can you live if you can't love? And how can you live if you *do*?

— James Baldwin, *Another Country*

I

The baby is twenty-four hours and seventeen minutes old. In celebration, I take a syringe of colostrum from the freezer and envelope it beneath my armpit. When the milk has melted to a liquid, I settle onto the sofa with the baby. I cup the back of his head in the palm of my hand, so that we are face to face, the rest of his body propped upright on my forearm. In this position, I can trickle the thick yellow milk from the syringe into his mouth. He swallows most of it, releasing only a small dribble from one corner of his lips. At the far end of the room, the windows have steamed over. The air in here is hot and wet. My skin slides against the baby's. Through the thin gaps in the shutters, I watch drops of condensation weave clean lines down the glass. It's July, and yet again the sun is coming up.

After the colostrum is all gone, I place the baby on my chest, his legs folded beneath him like a frog's, his neck turned so that one of his cheeks is squashed against my breast. He sleeps there for a while, digesting. I stay as still as I can so as not to wake him, listening to his irregular, shuddery breaths. I watch the light move on the ceiling. Sometimes the baby stops breathing, as if after this very short taste of living he has already changed his mind. These occasions last only a matter of seconds, surely, but they drag like hours. I hold my own breath in response, tensing my entire body so that I can focus completely on his. I wait like this, silently fighting my climbing urge to wake him, to remind him to take a breath. Each time that thin wheeze rises, finally, from his lungs, I am so relieved that I cry.

When the baby wakes, he cries too. He shows me real crying, so big and desperate it splits the room. In the middle of the noise, I notice a yellow oval of milk on his pink tongue. Back at the hospital, I found that if I stood, his tiny form pressed securely to mine, and rocked very hard, he'd stop crying. In the flat, I try this same trick. I am attempting to simulate the womb. But there is no fooling the baby. He wails and keeps on wailing. I slow my rocking. I hold him in my arms, hushing him, and watch the yellow oval continue to tremor on his tongue, his eyes screwed tight. I can't hear myself hushing, which means he can't either. I fear he will never stop crying. I fear he will never forgive me.

I decide to change his nappy. I lay him down on the floor, a muslin over the mat to protect his bare skin from the cool plastic. He continues to cry. I know why he's crying, and it's not because of a wet nappy. He's crying for something else, something I cannot give him. In my fluster, I pull one of the new nappy's sticky tabs so hard that it rips. At the sound of the rip, the baby stops crying. He opens his navy eyes, the irises thick as oil, and stares at me, affronted. Then his brow softens, and there is a look of such casual knowing, such tolerance, that a chill passes over me. He's biding his time, I can see that. He's decided simply to wait me out.

I'm not the baby's mother, and this is why he cries. He has no language to tell me that I'm not right for him, and yet he tells me with his body, with his eyes. I was naïve to think that, if I scooped him straight from the womb and held him immediately to my bare chest, so in his first breaths he would inhale only my smell, he would mistake me as his. I was wrong to think that, if I brought him home, all of time would be erased. In reality, the flat was just as we'd left it: the bath full with cool, blue water; Nim's clothes a twisted loop on the floor; the ice cube tray upside down in the sink.

As soon as I got home with the baby, I'd closed the shutters and turned the lights off again, making it like a womb, so that I might allow him to go backwards, just for a moment. So that we might pretend like she was here. Those hours in the hospital had gone on forever. The best part was the five minutes right after the birth: the ecstasy of the new life. Then Nim was taken away to be stitched up, and I paced the stark corridors with the baby while we waited, thinking of everything I would say to Nim once she and I were alone together, once she had slept a few hours, once things had calmed. It was clear to me, even there in the hospital corridors, that the baby knew who I was, or who I wasn't. He knew by smell, by taste, that I was not his mother. The baby is an animal, and I couldn't fool him even if I'd wanted to. I *had* wanted to, of course, but that was before. The moment I met him, any hope I'd had to deceive him melted away, and suddenly the truth seemed very beautiful. As I watched the birth, I too had felt myself opening.

I don't know when I realised that Nim wasn't coming back. It dawned on me slowly. I wasn't sure how long stitches were meant to take: fifteen minutes, half an hour? An hour passed before I went to speak to some-one. The nurses thought Nim was lost in the hospital, that perhaps she'd been sent back to the wrong room. I noticed that the little suitcase I'd packed for her, with a change of clothes and her toothbrush and her phone, was gone. I alerted the nurses to this. A hushed panic bloomed slowly, all around us. The baby slept. Finally the cameras were looked at, and in them Nim was seen leaving, just walking out of the hospital car park. She'd left in a pair of tracksuit bottoms and a ratty grey hoodie, still waddling slightly, a smear of blood on her right eyebrow.

After that, there were many questions for me. The questions came from the nurses, then the doctors, finally the police. Mostly I remember Nim's phone ringing out, and ringing out again. That regular trilling, over and over, then the answer machine. I left a message where I tried to sound calm, reminding her that she needed rest and support, having so recently given birth. I left another where I told her that I loved her, that I had always loved her but been slow to realise. I left another where I was crying so much that nothing I was saying sounded like words.

I told the police what I knew, which was that, by leaving, Nim was trying to keep her side of a promise. I told them that they could look for her if they wanted, but that there wasn't much use.

Nim has run away before, I said. And she's good at hiding.

They asked me about her family, and I lied that I didn't know. I was composed when I said all this. I didn't want to give them an excuse to think I wasn't stable enough to take the baby home. They had no reason not to let me, since it was down in Nim's pregnancy notes that I was her partner. Still, I could see the judgement on the police's faces, the way they scanned me for signs I was defective.

As soon as I was alone in the hospital room, I brought the baby's face to mine. I closed my eyes and breathed him in. He hadn't been washed, and on his rodent-soft scalp I could smell the inside of Nim's body. It's true that I'd expected the baby to come out a stranger to me, pristine as a Cabbage Patch Kid from a box. I'd thought that his birth would erase everything, would make me brand new. But as soon as I saw the baby, I recognised him. His face was so obvious, and no less astounding for that. He smelled plush and earthy, like moss, like someone who'd been alive forever. I felt that he was the only person who understood me, in that cold hospital, after Nim went missing.

I pleaded with the doctor to let me take the baby home, rather than stay another night in hospital. I felt sure that if Nim were to return, it would be to the flat. The doctor, recognising my predicament, and conceding that the baby was a good weight despite having been born early, eventually gave his permission.

Here, the baby has resigned himself to waiting. I cannot blame him, for I am waiting too. I want Nim back desperately. Her phone rings and rings. Into the answer machine, I tell her that I'm sorry, that I was wrong. I tell her that I want whatever she wants, but at the very least I need to know that she's safe. I tell her that the baby is not only healthy but magic, that I sense in him something supernatural. I laugh a little after that, nervously. Then I lose control, and ask her to come back. I beg her. I hang up and call again, to apologise for the previous message. I tell her she owes me nothing, I'm aware of that. But if she could just call, I say. If we could just talk?

2

I've wanted to be a mother for as long as I can recall. As a child, I had no friends my own age. At school, I preferred to play imaginary games with the younger kids in the playground. I'd be the kind matron of an orphanage, or the babysitter of a giant rabble. The little ones loved the attention of an older girl; they'd run up to me asking to play. I'd give them sticks and pebbles for their dinner, then put them to bed in the sandpit. It interests me, now, that I never played at being their mother. At nine years old, I liked to imagine myself as a gorgeous woman in my twenties, dressed in flared jeans with stars on the pockets and red cowboy boots. I didn't think it was possible to look that way and to have also carried a baby. Perhaps deep down I knew that my body would never become pregnant anyway, because of the three miscarriages my mother suffered, in quick succession, the year I turned six. In my child's mind, I was unable to separate that word – pregnant – from the image of a toilet filled with blood.

What was it that I liked about small children, when I was still a child myself? There were a few things. I found them cute, with their wispy hair, their cheeks full and springy as water balloons. I was heavy and thick-limbed, with coarse curls that stood outwards when my mother brushed them. I prized myself on my neat handwriting, and I enjoyed finickity hobbies, like cross-stitch or intricate colouring. I gravitated towards things and people that I found small and beautiful, as a kind of outsourcing. Another reason I liked babies and young children was because they liked me. I understood even then that we are born real, socialised over time to be polite. Therefore, it seemed obvious to me that being liked by younger kids meant something deeper than being liked by older ones. I had a knack for making the little ones laugh, for coming up with games that they enjoyed. I never felt more popular than when walking across the playground, swishing my hips in my imaginary flares, a line of small children following me like ducklings.

It should be said that kids my own age never thought much of me. I was slow at sports and shy in conversation, an only child of overprotective parents. Perhaps it was for this reason, initially, that I set my sights on the little ones, too proud and self-conscious to chase after friends who showed no interest in me. I was lonely at home, and wanted to feel myself surrounded. My parents loved me deeply, they love me still, but the main purpose I served as their child was to need them, was to make them feel capable. I noticed the rush of energy my mother got when I was sick, or when I'd had a bad dream. I remember her cold hands on my hot face, the mug of warm cinnamon milk she'd give me in the night. But I too needed a chance to prove that I was capable, that I was a person who could provide as well as receive. The little children allowed me to play this role, if only in our joint imaginations, if only for an hour.

After school, my parents would create small issues, just so that they could parent me. I hadn't drunk enough water that day; I had tight hamstrings; I was anaemic. They were constantly fussing over my diet, over my sleep. Though they were never pushy. If anything, they had low expectations of me. They required nothing outside the realm of normal. The problem was that normal could feel like a very tight space, and it only became tighter as I grew. My parents' love was like a smoke-filled room, the walls closing in. I'm aware that they never intended to make me feel this way, that any knowledge of this would hurt them. Simply, their identities – particularly my mother's, but my father's too – were so greatly consumed by being parents that they couldn't bear to set me free in the world. If I grew up and no longer needed them, who would they be?

But I did eventually find myself an adult. Desperate to claim my independence, to prove that I was grown, I ripped myself away. At eighteen, I moved from the suburb of Portslade into Brighton, renting a room in the house of a youngish couple with a daughter. My parents had hoped I'd go to university, but I knew that if I did I'd likely have to return home for the holidays, and this put me off. I could no longer stand the concern on their faces. The way that, on the rare occasion I went out at night, they'd leave their bedroom door ajar. When I got in, I'd find my mother sitting upright in bed with her glasses on. The light was honeyed, her face in it creased with worry. My father was a lump under the covers, snoring a thick growl. When I think of my mother, this is still how she appears to me: waiting up for me always, her door held permanently ajar in preparation for the inevitable moment when I should somehow fall out of my own life.

Instead of university, I got a job in recruitment. I'd found the work of trying to get a job so boring that I'd settled for the first thing I was offered, and now it was my work to find jobs for other people. The mundanity was excruciating, but I liked speaking to my clients on the phone. It emboldened me that they never saw my face. I'd comfort them about their struggles to find work, I'd reassure them that these days it was increasingly common. I'd put on an accent that was posher than my usual, and after I hung up I'd wonder if they imagined me as older than my eighteen years.

In the evenings, I'd spend time with the little girl I lived with. Her name was Connie. She'd taken an immediate liking to me, as children often did. I didn't play at looking after Connie, as I'd done back in the school playground. I was an adult then, and no longer in charge of the imagining. Connie controlled our games, and in them she treated me like an oversized doll. I'd lie down on the rug in her bedroom and she'd fasten every one of her hairclips into my hair, or draw all over my face with the smooth nibs of her felt tips. Sometimes she'd wrench my chin until my mouth opened, and then she'd push objects inside. A cold marble, a coin she'd shaken from her piggy bank.

Take your pills, she'd whisper to me. Take your pills and you'll be all better.

If I tried to speak, she'd silence me immediately. You can't talk, she'd say. You're almost dead.

Sometimes, in my evenings lying on the floor for Connie, I'd find tears sliding down the sides of my face, blocking my ear canals so I could hardly hear her shuffling around her room, gathering up supplies for our game. I didn't know why I was crying, and I didn't spend long considering it. The crying refreshed me somehow, and that was enough. It was a kind of nightly cleansing. Afterwards, Connie's parents would call her to the bathroom to brush her teeth, and I'd go downstairs to boil myself some two-minute tortellini. Now, when I think back to my very early adulthood, these moments with Connie strike me as some of my happiest. It seems to me that I was crying out of relief, rather than sadness. Relief to return, just for a moment, to a time in which I had no agency, no responsibilities for myself at all. Being with Connie resembled being with my parents, in that way. Lying on the floor while she drew over me like a piece of paper, I could give up on my tussle for independence. I could rest.

I spent three years living with Connie and her parents, then another five living alone in a rented studio flat above a chicken shop. For the most part, I remained the child I had always been: that unhelpful combination of proud and self-conscious; drawn to youth and beauty; prone to measuring my own success in terms of how useful I felt, how needed. It seems to me now that adults are just the children they once were, grown-up life not so different to the playground. Yet of course the stakes get higher.

3

In the office of the recruiting company, I met a woman named Christine. She was getting married. Though I didn't know her well, she invited me to her hen do. I was twenty-eight then, and despite my ten years in central Brighton, a relatively small city, I didn't have a lot of friends. I was flattered to receive the invitation. I remember thinking, on my way to the club, that this event was somehow the beginning of something. I was prone to thoughts like that; I suppose most unhappy people are. I wanted to live, I knew, but I still wasn't quite sure what that meant. I was seeing my parents more and more at this stage. I'd go round every Sunday, as well as once or twice mid-week. I had nowhere better to be. My parents would ask about my work, about my social life. They'd mention acquaintances of theirs who were becoming grandparents. They'd try to give me money, and I'd insist I didn't need it. It was true that I had savings, that I managed to put away a sum every month towards my far-off hope of buying a flat. I'd leave my parents' house with a full stomach, a heat spreading beneath the skin of my face that made me itch, and the dreadful certainty that I had failed, that I was failing anew with each passing day.

The club where Christine's hen took place had been open less than a year. It was called Gunk. The venue was grotty and popular, with Portaloos in the smoking area. There were large fog machines inside, so that it was mostly impossible to see who you were standing next to, and the air carried the distinctive scent of burning sugar. When I arrived that night, I found that half of the crowd knew Christine. She must have invited over one hundred people. I'd expected something more intimate; I'd expected to cultivate a few bonds. Instead, the entire smoking area was talking about her. I was not special to have been invited, that was clear to me from the moment I arrived.

Christine's maid of honour, who I can't now remember the name of, offered me some shrooms from a blue plastic bag. When I asked her what they were for she looked embarrassed and folded them back into the pocket of her jeans.

You must be Jules, she said. Jules from work?

People saw me as a square back then, which isn't so far off what I was. I'd told everyone in the office that my name was Jules, though really it was Julia; I'd never before used that nickname in my life.

I came to learn later that Christine's hen was one of the only nights ever held at Gunk in which most of the punters were over the age of twenty-five. Gunk was where Christine and her fiancé had first exchanged numbers, all those years before – though it'd had a different owner then, and a different name – and this was why the maid of honour had chosen the student club for her venue. The mood was relatively calm that night, far less raucous than I became accustomed to later. I think if it had been a usual event at the club, full of students picking fights and pissing themselves, I wouldn't have lasted five minutes. As well as that, Leon would've had a younger crowd to flirt with, and most likely would never have got around to me.

As it was, he and I caught eyes in the smoking area. He smirked using one side of his mouth. I didn't know whether he thought I was cute or ugly, but I knew it was one of those, because of the way his gaze lingered. I had a sharp chin, quick little eyes and hair in a pixie cut. My breasts were big enough to give me recurring backache.

Leon was smoking hash, and he gave me a toke. I knew better than to ask him what it was, after the incident with Christine's maid of honour. I put my mouth on the end as he lit it for me, let the smoke fill my lungs. Afterwards my eyes began to water, and I found it very hard not to cough.

Leon was wearing a T-shirt with a squiggly graphic that rippled against his skinny frame, and there was a fine ring of white dust around his left nostril. He was a small man, just under five-foot-five, and sinewy. He had a pussycat mouth and unruly eyes, his jaw so tight you could see the hinge of muscle along the bone. I asked him what he did for a living, once the tickle in my throat had passed. I couldn't think of anything cooler to say.

I run this club, he said. This place is mine.

I hadn't believed him, but I'd liked that he was trying to impress me. He took me inside and told the student behind the bar to make me a drink. There was a queue, but we pushed in front. What you having, then? asked the student.

Leon ordered a Jägerbomb.

I'll have the same, I stuttered.

The student fixed our drinks. They didn't ask for any money. The Jägerbomb tasted like cough syrup, and immediately afterwards I was drunk. I'd read some-where that Jägerbombs could kill you; apparently the alcohol slowed your heart while the energy drink sped it up, until your body got so confused it just gave out. I told Leon this, right after he'd knocked his back. He put his fist to his chest and spread his fingers wide, to demonstrate an explosion. I started laughing and found I couldn't stop. He was intimidating, but only in a way that made me want to remain near him. He had an aura which I hoped might rub off. He leaned in and kissed me. I wasn't expecting that. Hiccups of laughter kept coming up from the bottom of my throat into his mouth, and I was worried he thought that they were burps. After a minute or so I calmed down, and the kissing got better. His mouth tasted sweet and hot, with an edge of something rancid. After we kissed, his smile was garish. One of his front teeth was angled, just slightly, over the other.

How's your heart? he said.

That would have been cheesy from anyone else, but Leon had a way of pulling things off. He told me then about the hole in his heart, how he'd nearly died as a four-month-old baby. He spoke with such feeling it was as if he could actually remember the surgery, his mouth so close to my ear that his voice burned like an exhaust pipe. Of course I lapped it up.

Later I learned that Leon always told this story when he took cocaine. Over the years I saw multiple girls get teary as they imagined baby Leon hooked up to tubes.

The girls' hands would come to hover unconsciously over their own hearts, as if to protect them.

I don't get it, one of the girls said to me once. There's literally a hole through his heart, but it still works and everything?

I'd shrugged a shoulder. By that point, Leon and I had been married four years. Debatable, I'd said.

On the dance floor, Leon put his hands on my hips as if he'd known me for at least an hour. I turned around so I was facing away from him and started grinding on his crotch. I don't know where that move came from, somewhere very deep within me. Sometimes I could grope around inside myself and come up surprised. My forwardness thrilled him. When I looked back over my shoulder, a grin had cracked up his face. I was embarrassed, initially, and then I was pleased to have pleased him. I decided I wanted to please him forever. He was like a dog or a baby; being liked by him was chemical.

We kept dancing. The hash and the Jäger had a strong effect on me. I could feel a tingling in the backs of my eyelids, and every time I closed them I saw millions of pink sparks. When Leon invited me up to his flat, I nodded so vigorously I thought I might have pulled a muscle in my neck. He burrowed his face into my hair and clamped his teeth down on my earlobe. He was a little shorter than me, and I could feel him straining to get it.

We held hands while we walked. The streets milled with people stumbling home. In his scuzzy flat, Leon knelt between my legs and circled his tongue on my clit until the orgasm rose within me like a flare. There were full ashtrays everywhere, two or three in each room. I realised I hadn't told him my name. It's Jules, I said.

He asked me to stay over, and we slept on a mattress on the floor that was without a sheet. He was a troubled sleeper, at one point suffering a night terror so intense that he woke screaming, quivering and sweaty, with his limbs wrapped tight enough around me that I was unable to move. He was coming down off whatever combination of powders he'd been shoving up his nose that night. His skin felt clammy to the touch, radiated a smell like a peach too long ripe. I dabbed his damp forehead with my wadded-up T-shirt, raked my fingers through his greasy hair, and shushed him until he nodded off again.

In the morning, he was so asleep he looked dead. I wrote my number down for him on a Rizla, and let myself out.

4

Leon called a week later. When I heard his voice at the other end of the phone, I was stunned. For our first date, we went to the cinema. He bought a six-pack of beers en route and hid the cans inside the pockets of my puffer, as well as two in the hood. I was nervous that the person who checked our tickets would notice and deny me entry, but nobody seemed to care.

At the pick 'n' mix stand, Leon shoved far more scoops of gummy peaches into a paper bag than we could reasonably eat in the time it took to watch a film.

It's all about the peaches, he said. These other ones are pointless.

I peered at the little plastic troughs. What about Jazzles? I suggested.

Leon stuck a scoop in. You're right, he said. Jazzles have style.

Little compliments like that could bowl me over, coming from him. I'd have to bite my lip to stop myself from smiling.

Once we were in the screen, I don't think Leon ate a single sweet. He passed out and missed the first half of the film, snoring so loudly I had to keep grabbing his face and angling it in directions that meant he went quiet. When he finally woke up, he was horny. He started nibbling my neck and running his hands across my breasts.

In the end we went into the disabled toilets to have sex. I couldn't get wet at first – it was cold in there and it smelled like bleach – but I got into it eventually. The handrails made for good places to hold on to. When we kissed, I was aware of the layer of fur that the sugar had left on my teeth. I got dressed quickly afterwards, and we sucked down a couple of the beers. Someone knocked, and we opened the door to find a boy of nine or ten in a wheelchair and a middle-aged woman wearing a lanyard. As Leon and I walked sheepishly out into the brightly lit hallway, she looked at us with disgust. I still had the sweets in the paper bag, and I placed them on the disabled boy's lap, out of guilt.

Leon kissed me hard outside the cinema, his hand cupping the back of my neck, as the passing traffic scanned its lights over us. I think I might love you, he said. He was laughing, like it was a joke. I thought it probably was a joke, since we'd only just met. Still I let it hang in the air between us, warming me up. It was winter then, there was black ice on the roads.

I didn't see Leon for a year after that. I called him a few times, and got no response. Some days I didn't mind it; I told myself I was lucky to have had those small pieces of him. In the end I bit the bullet and turned up at Gunk, just walked right over and said hi. He didn't remember my name, but when I reminded him he lifted his hand to my mouth and brushed the middle of my bottom lip with his thumb, very lightly, as if removing a speck of lint. He told me he'd missed me.

It was Leon's idea to get married. By that point we'd been a couple for just under six months, living together for three. I'd learned that was how Leon was: he didn't have the capacity to wait, to think things through. If he did, he'd only get distracted. There was a twisted logic to it, but a logic all the same. He moved to nothing but his own desires, which could come to him at any moment. He'd taken over the club on a whim, backed by his blindly supportive mother, after his attempts to become a DJ had failed. By the time I met Leon, he'd nearly driven the venue into the ground. He asked for my help, and because I loved to be needed I quit my job at the recruitment centre and took on the role of bar manager at the club. I surprised myself with how much I liked the work. I was good at it, undistracted by all the shenanigans that went on in a place like that. On my watch, the business finally started to turn a profit.

Leon was drunk when he asked me to marry him, leaning against the outside wall of the club, one of his mucky trainers kicked out over the other. He booked the registry office right there, on his phone, his voice full of laughter.

Course I'm serious, he said. Have you met me?

There was a six-week wait for our appointment. We spent that time working at the club, eating crisps in bed, which was still just a mattress on the floor, and rewatching the same few episodes of *The Office*. I didn't really get the humour – those people just seemed normal to me – but I laughed whenever he did. To my surprise, when the date arrived, we showed up to the registry office. We caught the bus, Leon in his leather jacket, me in laddered tights and a tartan miniskirt. It was 2012 in Brighton, and that was how people dressed. Our witnesses were two members of staff from the club: Carlos, the bouncer, and Dana, the woman we employed to scrub the Portaloos.

I remember that Carlos in particular had a sad look on his face, almost apologetic. I hadn't bothered telling my parents I was marrying Leon. It didn't seem real to me, only a prank we were playing on ourselves.

Does a bear shit in the woods? said Leon, when the registrar asked him if he wanted to take me as his wife. I'd laughed at that. I'd given him a jokey slap on the arm. I thought he was being romantic, honestly I did.

Afterwards we went to the pub and each ordered a pint of Guinness. I sat across from Leon in the beer garden. He was holding a supermarket bouquet – pink roses that had already browned at the edges – and smoking a cigar. His jaw was so sharp you could have cut the stems on it. I felt lucky then. I felt I was finally doing that thing called living. When we left the pub I hung on to Leon's arm, worried that otherwise he'd float away.

We honeymooned in the Lake District, stayed in a tiny cottage and watched the rain stream down the windows. I built a fire out of logs that I found in a back shed, and Leon sat by it and melted down a plastic milk carton until the whole place was filled with black smoke. We did acid and lay on top of a green hill. I spent my whole trip trying to convince Leon that the crawling sensation he could feel on his skin was only the tickle of the grass, and not the legs of an endless colony of spiders. I held his head in my arms and stroked his forehead, like I'd done the first time we met. I was quite happy that day; I enjoyed seeing his body curled up like a woodlouse, enjoyed being able to offer him comfort. That evening, after the acid had worn off, I discovered a constellation of insect bites all up my back. They itched like mad.

5

In the beginning of my marriage to Leon, I obsessed over what our baby would be like, when it came. The day Leon introduced me to his mother, we watched hours of footage of him as a boy. Rita lived alone in a dark flat full of white pleather and crystal lamps, her fridge crowded with gaudy magnets. She chain-smoked cigarettes and plucked her eyebrows very thin, drew on her moles with liner. She'd been a model when she was young, and showed me an eighties editorial of her younger self in roller skates, her hair fluffed out. She showed me another in which she was naked except for a shearling jacket, a black thong and a pair of ski goggles.

I looked at Leon for signs of embarrassment, and found none. Rita still carried an air of celebrity, despite her cramped and musty flat. She appeared so used to being looked at.

Leon had been talking about introducing us for months, but Rita was often on holiday. She'd spend long weekends in Lisbon, in Rome. There, I imagined, she'd sit in squares and drink coffee, wait for local men to pick her up. She sent Leon a postcard from every trip, printing a kiss in lipstick instead of signing her name. I found that gross, almost sexual, though I understood also that it was glamorous, that it hinted at a blurred line, a youthfulness, which my parents would never have been able to carry. Rita hadn't had a serious relationship since Leon was small, when she'd called off her engagement because her son, at just five years old, had refused to allow the man inside the house. Leon had nearly died as a baby, due to the hole in his heart, and had been a sickly child after. Doubtless this was the reason Rita spoiled him. She would never have stayed with someone who her son didn't approve of, and this meant she stayed with no one.

Leon's my number-one boy, she told me proudly, that first day we met. As long as he knows that, I'm happy. I don't need another thing.

She set up a projector in her living room, for the home videos. Most of them were filmed when Leon was twelve or thirteen, which was when I supposed Rita had bought the video camera, and in them Leon was quippy and gorgeous, the kind of child who people imagine will one day become famous. In some of the videos he was filming, in others he was being filmed. I was happy to watch, considering at this point that I was infatuated with Leon, and therefore infatuated with the child he'd been, which seemed not so far from the child he would one day give to me.

In the video I remember best, Leon was filming Rita in what used to be their kitchen. Here's my mum, he said, holding the camera shakily, the zoom clicking as he drew the frame into her face. She was stood in front of the fridge, decorated with the same collection of magnets she had still, gathered from her modelling work abroad.

Not so close, said Rita, laughing. Please, Leon, not so close.

Leon continued to zoom further, so that for a second only Rita's left eye was in shot, then her cupid's bow, both things eventually losing focus and becoming pixels.

You're gorgeous, came Leon's not-yet-broken voice, through the blur. Isn't she gorgeous? Go on everyone, he said, speaking to his imagined audience. Tell her she's gorgeous.

Watching this video, I saw that the Leon I knew was already there, in this boy, fully formed. At twelve years old, he was both charismatic and exasperating, incapable of listening or of following instruction, yet somehow pulling this off and managing to delight his mother, whose coquettish laughter could be heard in the background, despite her wishes being again and again ignored. He was beautiful and brazen and bad with it. He loved attention in whatever form: positive or negative, it hardly mattered, so long as someone, anyone, was thinking about him. Leon was skilled at giving the impression, in a room full of people, that you were the one he'd picked out. His issue was longevity, resilience. There was something unquiet about him, I saw that straight away: a continuous internal buzzing that meant he grew bored of everything easily, including people.

In the beginning, this unquietness hadn't put me off, but the opposite. It had excited me. I was running from conventionality, from the pressure of the trajectory. My parents thought they were asking the bare minimum of me: to seek out a life that was happy, safe and normal. But it turned out that was not a simple thing to achieve, and somewhere along the line the pressure had caused me to buckle. So I'd married Leon, a man who I loved warily. From the start, I turned a blind eye to his regular absences, to the way he had of refusing to pick up the phone only to resurface again, without explanation, weeks later. I hung off his every compliment, I celebrated each text. I let him unspool me with a single wink.

When I look back, I see that our marriage was not really a union at all, but rather a marriage of individualism. From him I settled for no commitment, no consideration, no real care at all. He didn't ask me for too much, either. I focused on my work, put most of my time and energy into the club. He was never faithful to me for longer than a month, but I took six years to leave him. I thought that being married was easier than being single. Certainly it was cheaper, to live as one half of a couple. As well as that, and despite everything, I wanted my baby. I saw even then how depressing both of these reasons were, how devoid of revolution. Perhaps I'd been coached, as a woman, to expect very little from men, to give more of myself in a relationship than my partner, to see marriage as an endurance test rather than a mutually valuable way to pass my life. But at the same time I'd sought out wildness, I'd craved freedom, I'd invited mess. I'd been determined to secure a story that looked different from my mother's. It's true that I was no revolutionary. I was too weak to reimagine a life for myself, to rip apart the structures that had been set in place for me, to fully dismantle the architecture.

I was too scared, even, to go to the doctor for tests when I didn't fall pregnant. I knew that if my infertility were to be officially confirmed I would have to rethink my approach to motherhood, and I was petrified of that. Something of my parents' craving for normalcy lived on in me, and would not die. For years, the arrival of my period hit me like a brick in the chest, and I'd spend all day winded.

6

After Leon and I divorced, we continued to see each other most nights, at the club. There, I grafted tirelessly while Leon gallivanted around in his drainpipe jeans, his dirty white Converse with the biro scribbles all over, offering bumps of coke to students he had a crush on. Either he'd slope off home at the end of the night with one of them, or end up falling asleep in some dank corner, waking to find a stranger's coat thrown over him. By then, when I looked at Leon, I felt almost numb: all the anger and pain and love had finally ebbed away. Being married to him had exhausted me to the point that I had nothing left.

I had let go of Leon, yet my dream of motherhood clung on. I looked into adoption and IVF, but the scale of both routes seemed impossible: the hours of research required, the thousands of pounds, the injections and interviews and flights across the continent. All around me, people got pregnant by accident. On the bus, I overheard stories of failed contraception, of women who'd got pregnant via holiday romances with married men. I wanted it to happen like that. I wanted a whoopsie. Why should I have to fight for a child, all alone? I had given up six years for a bad marriage, and come out with nothing. The injustice of it withered me. My only hope was the club, the one place outside my flat that I regularly went. There, I supposed I might meet a man who'd take me home, who'd be irresponsible with contraception. It was not so unlikely an idea, and though I suspected I was unable to conceive, there'd been no actual tests to prove it. In the end, it didn't happen quite like that. But it wasn't so far off, either.

When I close my eyes, I can still picture Nim in the club, just as she was the night we first met. She's stood with me behind the bar, glass bottles lined up behind her head, her hair shaved to a velvet and her mouth big and wet and laughing, pulling in all the light in that humid, strobe-filled room. Now, I open my eyes and I see her son in my arms. If Nim never comes back to us, if she succeeds in disappearing forever, I'll describe her for the boy in this way, once he's old enough to understand, so that he can picture her just as she was, before all of it. So that he can look in the mirror and catch, in glimpses, the woman he came from.

The flat I rent is two blocks from the club, just up from the seafront, overlooking a kidney-shaped expanse of poured concrete in which large coaches of tourists park up in the summer. The flat is the most comfortable of all the places I've inhabited. Living with Leon wasn't much different to living in a squat. Everything was broken and grimy, all the furniture pulled off the street, and one of the windows never closed, meaning a continuous stream of freezing sea air was siphoned in all winter. My current flat is large for one person, with high ceilings and wooden shutters that create golden stripes of light. I have rugs on the floor, blankets thrown over the arm of the sofa. My mother gave me a cheese plant, and each week I dust the green heart leaves with a cloth to keep them shiny. Now, there's a bouncy chair on the floor, a playmat with toys that dangle, a blanket the size of a laptop. It turns out that I'm a homebody, on the condition that I like my home.

After I moved out of Leon's, I realised how important it was that I lived somewhere that felt markedly different from the club. I'd spent so many years between Leon's flat and Gunk, two places in which the soles of my shoes made a sticking sound every time I walked across the floor, where each and every surface was speckled with tobacco and flecks of weed, and in which the smell of rotten eggs wafted from every drain, the stench of piss from every toilet. The club was defined by its grottiness. The place was called Gunk, after all, and we owed our punters the thing that they asked for. At least that was the impression that Leon liked to give. In fact the dilapidation of the club was not due to stylistic choice so much as a lack of funds. Half the windows in the club were smashed and boarded over with cardboard, so inside it was often glacial. There was a tangle of wires behind the DJ booth that I refused to go near for fear of electrocution. The floorboards were rotting, and plaster fell like sand from the walls. Punters on the dance floor kept their coats on the whole time, oscillating for warmth. It was fortunate that the club only opened at night, since we relied on the strobe-lit darkness to hide the endless hazards, and the deafening speakers to drown out the sound of rats scratching in the walls.

Many of the students who frequented the club came from wealthy families. I suppose those who didn't were less likely to spend their nights on the lash, frittering away their parents' money. I'd overhear them talking left-wing politics in the smoking area, only to discover later that their parents were Tory MPs. I

kept an eye on the kids, in that way. I had my favour-
ites, the ones who would again and again catch my
eye. The students were in the time of their lives where
they sought out rebellion, the time before exhaus-
tion would make them weak or stress would make
them greedy. For now, they still had some energy.
They believed in things like horoscopes. They hated
the police, and they hated fossil fuels, and they hated
capitalism. For the students, the club stood in oppo-
sition to these things. The mess, to them, was proof
of lawlessness. It helped, of course, that they found it
fun to get fucked up and have a dance, that they had
money with which to buy a ticket and a pill and a few
shots of tequila. Gunk was a business, no matter how
well Leon attempted to hide it.

Leon himself was another of the club's hazards,
another symbol of transgression. To be seen with the
older, coked-up, spookily handsome manager of the
club – his ropey thumb hooked into the belt loop of
your jeans, his grey tongue in your ear – had an air
of the disgusting, the delinquent. It was this kind
of behaviour that the students craved, this that had
brought them to the club in the first place. Leon was
blind to many things, but he wasn't blind to that. He
had picked the club's name out himself. It was he who
hired students to work the bar, and he only hired those
he fancied. Even when we were married, he did that.

Especially when we were married, in fact. It was his way of keeping them around.

Anyone hired to work alongside me would soon notice that Leon didn't lift a finger. Sometimes the odd comment was made about this, though it was always light-hearted. I heard Leon referred to most often as a prince or a poser, both of which he took as compliments. I didn't care who he hired, so long as they showed up every night the rota required of them and didn't quit too quickly, as the students were prone to do. Most of them arrived in the city eager for work, but found themselves losing stamina after their first term. It wasn't easy to study and party and hold down a job all at once, particularly for kids who'd grown up with their own swimming pools, their own horse stables.

Leon had a type that I could pick out from miles away: fleshy and overly sweet, like the cherries at the bottom of the bag. I had been that way, though I didn't know it, when I first met him. Nim, however, did not strike me as a usual choice for Leon. I noticed her first around ten o'clock, when the club was slowly filling for the night. It was early winter then. She'd followed him across the dance floor towards the bar, where I was stood. She was far taller than Leon; lean and leggy as a new plant that hadn't got enough sun. Her gait was uneven, as if she'd just shot up overnight. This I supposed she could have, being that she was only eighteen years old.

Jules, said Leon. This is Nim. She'll be starting on the bar.

Nim lifted her eyes to me. She had a brief, initial shyness that I mistook for an attitude, but she had an attitude too, a steeliness that made me uneasy. Hi, I said.

Without smiling, she winked. That wink felt over-friendly, conspiratorial, and the sudden confidence of it put me on edge. Nim and I were not co-workers; I was her boss, she my employee, and I wanted that to be clear to her from the start. I flicked my eyes to Leon, to show him I had my doubts. I was used to the well-bred Disney stars that were his usual preference: clumsy chatterboxes who did everything I said for two months, then quit without warning because they had an essay due. Whether or not they ended up in bed with Leon, I hardly cared. Some of them did, some of them didn't. If they did, it would last a matter of weeks, no longer. They were only looking to satisfy some small rebellion in themselves, to do something they knew would horrify their parents. I saw little risk in it, low chance of lasting damage.

Nim, however, was harder to interpret. I couldn't look at her and predict how the next few months would unfurl, as I'd learned to do with the others. I didn't even know whether Leon fancied her. She seemed so far from his typical type. There was no chemistry between them that I could detect. Still, she was beautiful. That was something I couldn't deny. She had a strange, unlikely beauty: the kind of beauty that grew on you, that crept up and slapped you around the face. Her shaved head gave her a startling look. The wink she'd thrown me had seemed almost flirtatious, though I couldn't be sure.

7

The first thing I thought, training Nim for work, was that she didn't need training at all. She poured a shot like no one I've ever seen. I remember watching the vodka stream from the bottle: the way she raised the neck higher than her shoulder, judging it so perfectly that when she stopped pouring and brought the bottle upright again, the final drop landed in the centre of the shot glass like a bead of dew on a fish pond. Tiny ripples ricocheted out, catching in the blue strobes. I asked her if she'd ever worked a bar before, and she told me she had.

I started in the pub on the end of my road when I was fourteen, she said.

That can't be true, I said. That's not legal.

Nim only shrugged, like it made no difference to her what I believed. I looked old for my age, she said. And we needed the money.

Nim was wearing a zipped-up hoodie and had tiny hoops stacked in her ears, the cheap silver colour oxidised away. Her shaved head was smooth, almost foetal, and she had a small scar the size of a fingerprint on her scalp, just behind her left ear, where no hair grew. I figured she was telling the truth about the pub. There was no giggle in her voice, no desire to impress. She poured another shot, so we had one each, and together we washed them down. I didn't drink on the job usually, but it was a policy of mine to allow each new employee the first shot that they poured. I'd noticed that the alcohol loosened them up, ignited their confidence. I liked to give the impression, too, that I was generous. I hoped to get them on side.

I asked Nim where she'd grown up. She told me she was from the Midlands, but she didn't say exactly where. It was only then that I noticed the trace in her accent. I asked if she'd moved down here for university, and she shook her head. I'm not a student, she said.

This made sense to me, too. It wasn't only her accent that was different, but the way she spoke. She hadn't learned to pontificate, to babble. That was what all these kids really studied at university, I was sure: how to sound smart, whether or not they actually were. I was lofty about the fact I'd never got a degree, and secretly I preferred people who hadn't got one either. I wanted the lot of us to rise up and take control. I called the alternative, as in whatever I'd done, the University of Life.

What did you come to Brighton for, then?

I jumped a train south, she said. And this is as far as you can get.

Right, I said. When did you arrive?

A couple of months ago.

Without checking with me first, she filled her shot glass for a second time, and filled mine too. There was that cheek again, that sudden confidence. Her technique radiated it: the height to which she lifted the vodka bottle as she poured would have come across flashy from most people, gauche, but Nim moved with such casualness, such lilting ease, that she made pouring from so great a distance look almost normal. I eyed our second shots. I wouldn't have stood for that usually – my employees simply helping themselves – but tonight I let it slide. I did my shot, and Nim did hers.

You go home much? I asked.

She shook her head. This is my home now, she said.

I bet your parents miss you.

Nim looked at me, her eyes a flash in the dark. Her mouth was set straight. You don't know anything about them, she said.

I almost jumped back from her then; that look was like a knife. I had a gummy feeling in my mouth, toothless. I was prone to laughing at the students for their badly concealed privilege, the way they scuffed the newness from their shoes and dropped their Ts on purpose, yet I myself had been raised in the suburbs, an only child of two of the most placid, attentive people I'd ever known.

As fast as it had come, the grim look on Nim's face passed, and it appeared I was forgiven. How long have you worked here? she asked.

I shrugged, though I knew the answer exactly. A while, I said.

You like it?

I shrugged again. It's just my life, I said.

She laughed. Nice, she said. Inspiring.

Well, what do you want to do, in the long term?

She slid her eyes over the dance floor. Something like this suits me fine, she said. I like never having to get up in the morning, and I like leaving my work behind when I go home. Basically I just want to show up and get paid.

Then how're you ever going to get filthy rich? I asked.

Nim grinned. I'll rob the till when your back's turned, she said.

We hardly kept anything in the till, since most people these days paid with card. Still, I tried to make my face serious. I didn't want to give her any ideas. It was no use. Nim's smile was infectious, and soon I was grinning too. I was loose from the shots, and I surrendered easily. I liked this girl's company; I understood that already. I helped myself to a beer from the fridge. I offered one to Nim, and she accepted. I cracked the lids off with the opener that we kept tied with a string to the handle of a drawer.

The music got louder. Nim rolled her shoulders to it and bobbed her head. The night was set to be busy, a crowd already forming at the bar. I sipped my beer and doled out cans of Strongbow Dark Fruit to kids who already had a gurn on. Nim punched digits into the card machine and thrust it out with a practised arm. Despite it being a popular night, that shift was one of the smoothest I'd ever worked. The line at the bar was never longer than two or three people, and though Nim worked fast, she remained unflustered and full of humour. She kept up an easy rapport with the punters, leaning over the

bar so they could shout their orders into her ear, sliding their cans across the fake marble countertop as if
she was playing a game of air hockey. Nim slurped her
beers, swung her card machine, poured shot after shot
with her same outrageous technique.

8

We worked solidly for six hours, drinking all the time. I was alight with the alcohol, almost electric. When the music switched off, I thought there'd been some kind of fault with the speakers. It wasn't until the overhead lights flashed on and all the punters started to clear out that I realised the end of the night had come around so soon. Carlos, the bouncer, came inside to gather up the final stragglers. He was wearing a big coat and a wool hat and a pair of mittens, having spent all night stood on the street outside. The lights were over-bright, a little dazzling, picking up all the dropped lighters and hoop earrings and emptied baggies scattered across the pounded matt floor.

That's one way to get people out of here, I guess, said Nim, squinting into the bleak expanse. She sprayed the bar down and began wiping it with a rag. I noticed the pepper of mascara dusted beneath her eyes, the blackheads mixed in with the freckles on her nose.

You look tired, I said.

She raised an eyebrow. Thanks, she said, all sarcasm. Sweet of you to say.

I just mean that was a long night, I said. You did well, though. Thank you.

Nim looked at me for a while. I felt, under that look, as if I hadn't met anyone's eyes in years, not properly. Let's go for breakfast, she said.

It's four o'clock in the morning.

Nim was pulling on her coat. Alright, she said. What meal is this, then? Dinner?

I've got to get home, I said.

You don't eat?

I'll eat when I get up.

By then you'll definitely have missed breakfast. It'll be lunch, at least. Come on, I know a place on the seafront that's open all night.

Are you taking me to Buddie's?

She grinned. I forgot you were local, she said.

Nim had got my coat from the hook now, and she was holding it opened out so that I could slip my arms in. I felt pleased that Leon hadn't come back to claim her, as he so often did at the end of the night with the girls he hired. Just as I thought that, he appeared. Leon had a knack for showing up exactly when he wasn't wanted, and never once arriving when he was expected to. Now, he sauntered in through the main door, almost tripping over himself, an unlit rollie hanging from his lip. There was a thin, yellow light coming down from the streetlamp over the smoking area, and in the frame of the doorway his gaunt face looked angelically lit, close to haunting. Once he was through the corridor and in the main room with us, the overhead glare showed him as he was: sickly, with heavy bags under his eyes. He walked over, hands in his pockets, and leaned into the bar. He fished a lighter from the depths of one pocket, sparked it and started to smoke. Nim and I stood on the other side of the bar with our coats on, waiting for his next move.

Girls, he said.

He was off his face, I could tell by the way he spoke that single word. He tried to look at me, but his eyes wouldn't focus. He turned his fuzzed-out gaze on Nim. You're a natural, he slurred.

Nim's stare ran cold. I have five years' experience, she said. You've seen my CV.

He raised his eyebrows, a smirk on his face, shocked at the assumption that he ever would have read it. Alright, he said. Was only tryna pay you a compliment. You're a professional now, are you?

Nim sniffed. It was clear to me what had happened here: she'd flirted with Leon previously, in order to land the job, and now that she'd secured a position and proved herself skilled at it, she'd frosted over. It was a tale as old as time.

Leon looked between us, appearing to finally register our coats. You two seem like you're getting on, he said. Leaving together, huh?

I rolled my eyes. He was so predictable, it was stupid. Rather than accepting the reality of the fact Nim didn't want to sleep with him, it suited Leon better to imagine that I had somehow poisoned her against him, out of spite.

Just watch yourself, he said to Nim. She's cold as ice, this one. She can break a heart clean in half, if you let her.

Nim appeared to like this information. She looked at me, a smile flickering on her mouth. Sounds like gossip, she said.

I shook my head then, more to myself than either of them. That man would have rewritten all of history, blind drunk, if it meant impressing some girl he barely knew. Come on, I said. Leon, you can lock up. You're capable of that, aren't you?

Nim and I strode out of the club, leaving Leon slouched over the bar, composing a text on his phone. Double-check your spelling before you send that, I called back to him. Especially if it's for your mother. You'll worry her, Leon.

You wish I was texting my mother, he shouted back.

I do, as a matter of fact.

Nim and I stepped out of the club. The wind was biting. As I buttoned my coat, I scanned the smoking area — two Portaloos, chained to the metal railings in the corner; Carlos's plastic chair, where he sat late at night to rest his legs, tucked in by the exit; and beneath my feet the crunchy gravel, made up by now of at least sixty per cent fag ends — to conclude that nothing was out of place.

What's going on there, then? asked Nim.

With Leon? We've been divorced five years. He's a bastard, if you hadn't noticed.

Nim laughed. I would've thought anyone would notice that, she said.

You'd be surprised.

9

Buddie's, a twenty-four-hour greasy spoon on the seafront, was crowded with a mix of clubbers and taxi drivers, all seated at red-and-white chequered tables to eat fried mushrooms and fried bread and rashers of bacon. Nim and I ordered tea and fried egg sandwiches and took a seat in the far corner, huddled over our steaming mugs to get warm. I could taste the salt on my mouth from the walk over, carried on the wind that had been roaring down the promenade. Nim and I had walked bent into it, our coats billowing out behind us like sails. I couldn't hear anything over the roar, the waves crashing onto the pebbles below us, and neither could she. Unable to chat, we'd only glanced at each other, shyly, every time we passed under the light of a streetlamp. I hadn't noticed the shyness between us before then, and yet when I sat down opposite Nim in Buddie's I found myself unable to speak. She was quiet too. We perused the menus seriously, and then I got up to order. I guessed we were tired, finally, or sobering up.

When the teas arrived, I wrapped my numb fingers around my hot mug and left them there until the skin felt close to blistering. Nim emptied three or four sachets of white sugar into hers, her spoon clattering against the china as she stirred. Our sandwiches came soon after, and I squeezed ketchup from a giant plastic tomato.

So, she said finally. You broke his heart?

There was yolk on the corner of her mouth. He cheated on me, I said. Over and over again, in plain sight, until I finally gave up and left him.

Ah, said Nim. But *you're* the heartbreaker.

I gave her a look, then bit into my sandwich.

No kids? she asked.

No kids.

We were quiet for a beat. I want them, I admitted. Or, I want one. One would do me fine.

Nim nodded. You seeing anyone?

I shook my head. Even if I was, I said, I don't think I can get pregnant.

I'd not told anyone this out loud before, and I surprised myself when I said it. Sucks, said Nim.

I lifted a shoulder, let it drop.

My friend Beth's mum did IVF, said Nim, back when I was in school. I remember she kept her hormones in the fridge. I went in there once looking for yoghurt, and found a bunch of needles on the top shelf.

Did it work? I asked.

Nim bit her lip. Not that time, she said. But it did eventually. She went to Spain in the end, had a set of twins. I guess it's cheaper there.

I nodded. Happily ever after, then, I said.

Nim blew some air out her cheeks. I don't know about that, she said. Her husband was cheating on her the whole time, and she only found out when the twins were four weeks old. She kicked him out, but she'd had a caesarean, and she could hardly walk, plus she had two tiny babies to look after. She hadn't even wanted more kids in the first place; she already had Beth and Beth's older brothers. It was her new husband, Beth's step-dad, who'd been so keen, and he was the one who'd had the money for it. Then suddenly she had five kids, and no one around to help her out.

Jesus, I said.

Yup, said Nim. After that, Beth was so scared of getting pregnant that she made me come with her to the sexual health clinic to get an IUD inserted. We sat around for hours, and when it was done I had to practically carry her home. I guess the IUD rejected or something, because Beth bled like hell, and two weeks later her boyfriend literally pulled it out when he was fingering her. He held it up to the light, like: *what the fuck is this?* It must have hurt, but Beth said she didn't even flinch. She'd seen her mother's half-healed caesarean scar, so she knew what real pain looked like.

I winced.

Sorry, said Nim. I'm not sure why I just told you all that. I guess you make me nervous.

She took a bite of her sandwich, watching me while she chewed. I was smiling a bit. I found her curious. Nervous, I said. Why?

She shrugged, not taking her eyes off me. I dunno, she said. You have a presence.

I scoffed. No I don't, I said.

Nim slicked the spilled yolk from her plate with a finger and sucked it off. I find myself wanting to impress you, she said.

I laughed again. I suppose I am your boss, I said.

That's true.

I frowned, smiling still. The idea that this girl cared what I thought of her surprised me. How come you shaved your head? I asked.

Her sandwich was finished, her tea half drunk. I dunno, she said. I like the feel of it.

Don't your ears get cold?

Freezing, she said.

I went up to the till to pay. Nim tried to go halves, but I refused her. There was an ostentatious cream cake on a plastic stand on the counter, glacé cherries balanced on piped whorls of icing. I had a sudden urge to buy her a slice to take home, but I suppressed it.

Outside, the wind had died down, and dishwater light was creeping into the sky. The sun hadn't yet peeked over the horizon, and the sea was black.

You free to work tomorrow night? I asked Nim.

Sure, she said.

Just promise me one thing. You'll stay away from Leon, won't you?

She folded her arms. You jealous? she asked.

There was a glitter in her eye, and I knew she was playing. No, I said.

I'm kidding, Jules.

I know. I'll text you the rota in the morning. You need much work?

She nodded. This is all I've got on right now, she said. I'll take as many shifts as you have.

I'll be in touch.

I wasn't sure what had brought this sudden formality over me, what had made me bring up work at five o'clock in the morning on a miserable seafront, and I could see that Nim was wondering too. What followed was an awkwardness, some uncertainty about how we were going to say goodbye. Nim was stood with her head pulled in slightly, her brows low over her eyes, just watching me.

You'll be alright getting home? I asked.

I'm just up here, she said, nodding towards the cinema.

I could walk you, I suggested.

Is that because you feel responsible for me?

I was thrown off by that. I rolled my lips together and remembered my comment earlier, about her parents. I understood how irritating it was to be treated like a child, when you saw yourself as fully grown. I dithered for a moment, an apology on the tip of my tongue, and she took my dithering as me trying to decide whether or not to give her a hug. She opened her arms and folded them around me. Perhaps she liked me again, I didn't know. Our big coats squashed against each other. The hug was so brief that I picked up on no warmth from her body underneath.

Afterwards, she dropped her arms, but didn't step back from me. We were stood so close I could see the faint, downy hairs on her neck beneath the street lights. I could feel her eyes on me, but I couldn't meet them. I floundered like that for a while, waiting for her to say something, to turn away from me. I still didn't know whether or not I was walking her home. When I finally met her eyes, a smirk passed over her mouth, and she gave me a look like she knew exactly what I was thinking, and that she disapproved of the fact I couldn't simply speak aloud whatever that was. But I didn't know what I was thinking; I had absolutely no idea. I only blinked, vaguely startled, then mumbled some final goodbye and took off home.

I O

On Nim's second shift, she was withdrawn. It was as if she'd turned away from me, inside her mind, so that all her actions and conversation became gently muted. When she poured a shot, she didn't lift the bottle as high as she had the night before, and when she took payment for a punter's drinks, she didn't thrust the card machine out to them with quite the same impact. Still she worked just as hard as she had on her first shift, still the queue was kept to a minimum and still she smiled casually at the students as she took their orders, her movements fast but not rushed. If she'd been any other of my employees, I would have been pleased with her performance. But she was not another of my employees, and I could tell she was acting different.

When Nim had arrived at her shift, she'd asked me how I was doing. I'm sure whatever I'd said in response wasn't of much interest – probably I'd been working on my laptop that afternoon, sending emails and making phone calls on behalf of the club, as I did every day – but when she didn't reply, I'd wondered if she'd heard me. I'd waited for a minute or so, trying to make eye contact with her, but she was opening a box of plastic cups and lining them up on the back of the bar, and didn't look at me. Eventually I asked her what she'd been doing, and she told me she'd been asleep all day. She said it with no animation, as if it was neither funny nor strange that she might have slept for an entire sixteen hours since I'd seen her last. She spoke in a very flat tone, nothing but that single word: *sleeping*. I felt stung, and I didn't say anything more after that.

The first shift I worked with Nim, the night before, remains one of the greatest in my memory. This was not because of our efficiency when working side by side, but rather because of the energy she'd stirred in me. The only other shifts I can think of in which I experienced that same rush, that same springiness, were the first one or two that Leon and I worked together, back when we were newly married. It was always chaotic working the bar with Leon – it was often frankly ridiculous – but in those early days I'd loved just being near him. I was still so amazed that he wanted me around. I remember one time that he cut his hand open slicing limes, and he bled all over the chopping board and the black marble. Some students were screaming, and Leon was screaming too. I found an old first-aid box stuffed in the dark recesses under the sink and cleaned his wound and bandaged him up, and afterwards he nestled his slippy face into my neck and just sobbed there, for ages, saying the citrus was stinging, while I held him and the queue at the bar grew longer and longer. Ours was not a healthy marriage, and I would never claim that it was, but these small moments did generate some vitality in me.

I kept stealing glances at Nim that night, waiting for the forgiveness to come down over her face, the reveal of some great and hilarious joke. But she didn't look back at me, not really, not in the way that she had the night before. As an employee she remained polite, even thoughtful. If she needed something and I was in the way, she would rest her hand lightly on my shoulder until I moved. At one o'clock in the morning she made me a coffee, using the beat-up machine we kept under the bar, asking me how I took it and fixing it that way. I noted that she was using the same formality on me that I had used on her, in the early hours of yesterday morning, when we'd been stood on the seafront outside Buddie's and I'd found myself talking about the rota. She was showing me how it felt.

It was three o'clock in the morning, or thereabouts, when Nim went to the toilet and caught Leon's wrist as she was on her way back to the bar. The queue had died down by then, and a reasonable percentage of the crowd had already left, so there was a clean window from the bar through to the far wall of the dance floor. In that window, I watched Nim and Leon stand very close together for a moment, her hand latched to his. I watched them lock eyes, and I watched her pull him slowly towards her, as if she was going to whisper something into his ear, and then I watched them kiss, and keep kissing, their lips parting and running into each other. They kissed for a minute, maybe two, their eyes closed and their mouths churning very slow, while I just stood and watched, hardly even blinking, frowning in the half-dark, hoping that the image would eventually expose itself as no more than a trick of the light, and knowing that it wouldn't.

Nim had promised me less than twenty-four hours before that she would stay away from Leon. She had seemed so sure. What had changed? I hadn't seen the two of them share a single word that night. In fact, when Nim had first caught Leon's wrist, before the kiss, he had looked as surprised as I was. Now, his tongue glinted through the dark like a slug in a moonlit garden. Her shaved head was an orb, splitting a red strobe into a spray of smaller beams. There was no mistaking them, nor what they were doing. Then it was done, and she broke away from him. She journeyed through the crowd and back to the bar, stepped behind it like nothing.

What the fuck was that? I said.

For the first time all night, she looked at me properly. What was what? she asked.

When the club was closing and the lights came up on the dance floor, Nim slipped her coat on and paced over to Leon. He simpered when he saw her there, pleased with himself. Nim looked top-heavy with her big puffer and long, graceless legs. Their height difference was drastic, with Leon standing almost a head shorter than Nim, but Leon's confidence made up for this: the way he swaggered out of the club, popping the collar on his jacket as he went, swinging his neck back to check she was following. It took everything in me not to run out after them. Instead I filled a plastic cup with tap water and drank it down. The liquid tasted metallic, like blood, and once it was drained I filled another and sipped more slowly. I understood by then that Nim had intended for me to see the kiss, and also for me to see them leaving together. The only reason I could think of to explain why was that she was annoyed about my offer to walk her

home the night before, that she felt I'd been overbear-
ing. Her kissing Leon was, I theorised, an effort to show
me that I had no control over her movements. I couldn't
blame Nim for wanting to exert her independence, for
wanting to prove her life as her own. Though I didn't
appreciate her method, I could see the rationale behind
it. At her age, if I'd had the courage, I would've behaved
the exact same.

I wiped down the bar alone. I got the broom out and
swept the rubbish from the dance floor, leaving it in a
grisly pile in one corner of the big, cold room. When I
looked up from my sweeping, Carlos was stood in the
doorway, filling it almost completely, so the night came
in around his shoulders and large, meaty head.

You alright? he said.

Yeah. Tired.

Night off tomorrow, at least.

Oh, I said. Sunday. I'd forgotten.

You work too hard.

You can say that again.

You work too hard.

I gave a weak laugh. Carlos was full of little cracks
like that. He was a nice guy, nothing more. You wanna
go for a drink? he asked. Tomorrow, I mean. Some place
civilised.

I blinked at him. You mean like a date?

He shrugged. If you want, he said.

I'd known Carlos ten years at that point, and we'd rarely spent time together away from the club. I knew that he had a young daughter, that his wife had left him for somebody else a few years before. I knew that he'd been born and raised in Mexico, and spent all his savings on a one-way ticket to the UK when he was twenty-three. He spoke with an American twang, because he'd taught himself English by watching *Friends*. I agreed to the date, maybe as a reaction to Nim's betrayal, maybe because I was pleased to have been asked.

I I

I met Carlos the following evening, at a cocktail bar a few blocks from the club. There were garish frozen margaritas in slushie machines, and our drinks were served alongside a bowl of Twiglets. We drank tequila sunrises with dinky umbrellas in them. Carlos was a big man, and seeing him with that drink was comical.

My daughter's got glue ear, he said. She needs grommets.

Is that a surgery?

He nodded. His ex had recently had another baby, so it was Carlos who'd have to escort his daughter to the hospital.

I'm sure she'll be fine, I said. It's pretty common, isn't it?

He nodded. Oh yeah, he said. Jacinta's tough.

That's a pretty name.

Thanks, he said. It means hyacinth.

Carlos invited me back to his flat, after our drinks. He was rolling the umbrella between the pads of his thumb and forefinger, not looking at me. On the walk to his car I accidently burned him with the end of my cigarette. The burn left a scar, I noticed at work months later: the skin pastel pink as a carnation.

Carlos drove a black Mercedes, impeccably clean, an air freshener shaped like a pine tree dangling from the rear-view mirror. We were quiet all the way. The roads were near empty, and his driving was so smooth I was almost lulled to sleep. We took the coast road east, turning off when we reached the marina. Carlos rented a room in the poky new-build of a couple who'd retired early, moved to the sea and taken on a tenant to help pay their living costs. Everything in the house was boat-themed: the curtains and cushions striped white-and-blue, embroidered with tiny red anchors. I went straight up to his bedroom, and five minutes later he came upstairs with a plate of chalky crackers, a sliced apple and a block of cheddar. He gave me a glass of rosé that tasted like juice. He didn't partake in either the wine or the cheese, instead ripping the wrapper from a protein bar and eating the entire thing in three bites. Carlos was a gym rat, a man who steamed all his chicken breasts at the beginning of the week.

We talked for a while, about the motivational podcast he was listening to, and after perhaps fifteen minutes, he placed his hand on my knee. He picked up the chopping board and put it on his dresser, then he took my wine and put it there too. He kissed me, his tongue too big for my mouth. I could feel his heart beating through the meat of his chest, like a mouse I'd rescued from a trap when I was child. I'd put the mouse in a cardboard box in my wardrobe, with the inner tube from a toilet roll and a handful of peanuts. When I'd gone to check on the mouse an hour later, I'd found that it had died from the shock. I tried to stop thinking of this, and kept kissing Carlos. I considered how much easier my life would be if I was attracted to him. Don't think about that either, I said to myself.

The sex was fumbly. Carlos didn't have Leon's confidence, and nor did I. A part of me hoped that he would at least get me pregnant, but he got out a box of condoms that were scented in all different synthetic fruits and selected some kind of citrus: grapefruit or lime. There was a streetlamp right outside his bedroom window, so the light in the room was orange.

Afterwards, we were both sweating. I shuffled away from him and sat on the end of the bed, one of my legs crossed over the other, for some breathing room.

That was nice, he said. You're very beautiful.

I told him thanks.

I remember the first time I ever saw you, he said.

You do?

He nodded. It was the first night you came to Gunk, he said. You were on a hen. You were wearing a black top that tied in a bow at the back of your neck. Your group were the first people I hadn't had to ID in months. I clocked you right as you walked in, and I planned to ask for your number when you were on your way out. I was working up the courage. Next thing I knew, you were leaving with Leon.

I sniffed. How many times has that happened to you? I asked.

Carlos didn't miss a beat, didn't pause to think. Just the once, he said.

I thought he was a phony romantic; I didn't buy any of this for a second.

They're so young, he said. All these girls. I see them and I think of my daughter, it makes me sick. Leon's one fake ID away from a prison sentence.

I raised an eyebrow. And whose fault would that be? I said. Yours, for letting an underage in. Nothing's ever Leon's, that's for sure.

Outside the window, the bulb in the streetlamp flickered gently. I shivered, though I wasn't cold. Why did you stay with him so long? asked Carlos.

I shrugged. I'd dreamed of a family, and no matter how unsuitable a father I knew Leon would make, I hadn't been able to let my dream go. I didn't tell Carlos this, because of what it revealed about me. Any self-respecting person would have filed for a divorce years before I did.

What made you become a bouncer? I asked instead.

I'm big, he said. Big and stupid. I didn't have a lot of options.

You're not stupid, Carlos, I said.

I got up, suddenly irritated, and went to the bathroom. I gulped some water from the tap, then used Carlos's toothbrush and paste. In the pot, there was another tube with Peppa Pig on it, and without wanting to I pictured Carlos in here, bent low to scrub his daughter's molars.

12

Gunk didn't open again until the night of our weekly event, See You Next Tuesday, which was really only an excuse to print the word CUNT onto the back of each student's hand as they entered, using a custom-made stamp that Leon had ordered online. I got to the club early, having bought a falafel from the kebab shop opposite. Leon had an ongoing feud with the owner there. He thought the place owed all its business to the club, due to the foot traffic of drunk and hungry students we created. He'd charged in there multiple times, drunk and hungry himself, to demand a free meal on this basis. The manager had repeatedly declined Leon any free food, and had eventually gone so far as to ban him from the shop. I thought the ban was warranted, though mostly it had come to mean that whenever Leon wanted a kebab, which was often, he'd send me to collect it on his behalf. If I'd been Leon's mother, I'd have refused to buy anything for him in there until he'd sidled into the shop, his tail between his legs, and apologised to the owner. But Leon was not my son, and he didn't listen to a thing I asked of him. Besides, I'd long given up hope of making him a better person. Instead, I chose an easy life.

That night, I ate my falafel sat on a bar stool in the club, the floodlights making the pink and yellow pickles glow. Nim was working that night, and though I was expecting her, still when she walked into the club I felt a weight in my chest, like I'd swallowed too big a mouthful.

Hey, she said.

Hey.

You got a falafel?

Yeah.

Nice.

Neither of us spoke for a time. I was self-conscious of the sound of my chewing, so I put a hand over my mouth. Look, Jules, said Nim. I'm sorry about the other night. I never should have gone home with Leon. That was a bad idea. I don't know what came over me. I'm not even into men, usually.

It's fine, I said. It doesn't matter.

Nim cocked her head to one side, her eyes searching. You sure? she said.

I shrugged. Leon's fucked most of the women I know, I said.

Nim reached into her pocket and pulled out a Cornetto. I got you this, she said. For the ice queen.

I scoffed. It's November, I said.

I'll put it in the freezer if you don't want it now. You might later tonight.

I'd never eaten an ice cream after midnight before, but I watched as she paced over to the deep freeze and dropped it in with the big bags of ice. I felt immediately buoyed by her gift. I tried not to smile and couldn't. Well, I said. Thanks.

Nim was right; I did want it later. The club filled to capacity, and all that body heat made the room humid. Nim and I worked so fast we barely had a chance to speak. I got the Cornetto out at two in the morning, and stayed behind the bar to eat it. Nim gave me a thumbs up. What did I tell you? she said. She'd stripped down to a crop top, and there was sweat on her temples.

We were so busy that I couldn't take a real break to eat the ice cream. I had to keep putting it down on a paper napkin on the back shelf of the bar so that I could serve drinks. It was melting fast. Have some, I offered Nim. Help me with it.

By the time she picked up the Cornetto, the ice cream had melted to a liquid, and she had to drink it from the cone. I laughed while she did that.

We should put a shot of rum in, she said.

There was ice cream all over her hands, dripping onto the floor. The strobes flashed yellow, and in that moment she could have been on a summer beach, her face bathed in sunshine. She asked me if I was done with the Cornetto, and I nodded that I was.

You sure?

Yeah, I said.

Without moving her eyes from mine, she closed her hand into a fist around the ice cream, quite casually, and because the cone had softened by then to the point where it was only just holding together, it collapsed like wet cardboard, folded in on itself.

She beamed. That was so satisfying, she said.

She dropped the mess into the bin, flicked her hand over it a couple of times, then washed herself off in the sink. I looked at the floor, where five or six white drops of cream made a line to the bin. This is a scene that has never really left my mind, for some reason. Right now I can close my eyes and it's as if I'm actually there in the club, watching Nim flatten an ice cream to nothing, just to see how it would feel. I recognise this move, now, as typical of Nim, though when it happened I didn't know her well enough to see. It's this way she has of leaning into an impulse, then following it through to the end.

13

A bell rings, and I'm not in the club with Nim any more but in the flat with the baby. The bell is my buzzer. I rush to answer, and it is only when I hear my mother's voice through the crackle of the speaker that I remember my parents called an hour ago to ask if I was ready for a visit. How is it that I forgot, in so short a time, that they were coming? For a second, I presumed the person ringing the bell was Nim. The feeling now is like walking upstairs and thinking there's an extra step at the top of the flight. Maybe it would be funny, if there was someone else here to laugh. Nim would laugh, certainly, at something like my thinking there's an extra step. She's a fan of slapstick humour, and always loved it when I made a fool of myself. Now, there's no one here but the baby.

My parents, packed into the lift, slide very slowly up the building towards us. I can't tell if they're taking a long while to get to my door or not. With the baby, time feels slippery, full of warps. I can lose three hours walking between rooms with him in the sling, too afraid to sit down in case he wakes. Other times, a single minute of him crying will drag for so long that I swear I can feel myself inching, with each second, towards death. Being with the baby has got me thinking about death a lot. Every new life born is a new death in the world, at least eventually. I'm afraid that Nim will die, out there on her own with nowhere to go, leaking blood into maternity pads, her breasts swelling with milk that, if not expelled, could lead to sepsis. She's been gone two nights now, and I've no idea where she's slept, if she's slept at all. I'm grateful it's summer, at least; the days long and the nights warm.

My parents arrive with sunflowers, a knitted dinosaur with a bell inside it, and a plushie rabbit comforter that has a small square of muslin instead of a body. My mother scoops the baby up like he belongs to her and walks about the room with him, exaggerating her movements. I don't know how she knows that he likes being bounced. She's easy with him, much easier than I am, and seeing that makes me imagine myself as a baby. Again time goes lax, appears to stop for a second and unspool, and I can't understand how it is that I've sped far enough through my life to find myself here, with a child who is not mine but almost, my mother bouncing him on her breast.

I've been holding the baby constantly, even in sleep, and it's nice to have handed him over for a second. I stretch my arms above my head and then I swing down and reach for my toes. My spine cracks, as well as one of my knees. Suddenly it's inconceivable to me that I was ever a baby, that I grew inside my mother and was pushed out. I remember reading in a pregnancy book that a baby is born with almost one hundred more bones than an adult, that as we age they fuse together. I look at the baby now, with my mother, and think about how he has more bones, in his tiny body, than she has in hers. The impossibility of that. I think about how his bones were made inside of Nim. The impossibility of that, too. I remember the first time I saw the baby's bones, at Nim's twenty-week scan. They were bright against the dark of Nim's womb: lightbulb skull, glowstick ribs. I'd loved him already, I knew that, but seeing him had made it different, made it concrete. Nim wasn't looking. I remember that, too. She'd kept her eyes cast down the entire time.

For the first fifteen minutes of my parents' visit, my father hides in the kitchen, trimming the ends from the sunflowers and filling a vase, calling out offers of tea or coffee. My mother's wish to be a grandmother meant that she came around to the idea of my raising Nim's baby relatively fast, but my father has been more resistant. Doubtless he wonders why I couldn't just find a man and do it the old-fashioned way, like everybody else. Doubtless he wonders what's wrong with me. After I broke the news about Nim and her pregnancy, all he could talk about was the paperwork. He wanted to understand the legalities. I told him what I knew, which was that I could be listed on the birth certificate at the registry office some weeks after the baby was born, but that until the papers were delivered Nim could change her mind at any time. I had no rights, essentially, but this was my best shot at motherhood, perhaps my only shot, and I was willing to take the risk. Of course I was afraid that Nim would change her mind. But that was parenthood, wasn't it? Fear was the touchstone.

At this last point, my father had made a small hum of agreement and nodded his head. My parents are not imaginative people. They struggle to conceive of even the most basic diversions. When I first met Leon and told my parents he ran a club, they'd assumed that I was talking about a members' club of some kind. They'd enquired about a spa in the base-ment, a tennis court in the grounds, a swimming pool on the roof. These were the sorts of places that my parents had hoped I was inhabiting. They've never set foot in a private members' club, but they've read about them, in the context of seedy politicians, in the news. A nightclub, to them, may as well be the moon.

My parents smell so strongly of fabric conditioner that being with them is like being inside a stock photo of a blue field. In their house, they keep the heating cranked up to the point that the red circles on the high points of their cheeks have become permanent. When I go there for dinner, we sit in the same config-uration that we sat in all through my childhood, and my mother serves the exact same dishes she always has: exclusively meat-based, always accompanied by overboiled carrots and broccoli in the same blue china bowl. There is a specific schedule: roast chicken on Sundays, shepherd's pie on Wednesdays. The last Friday of every month, my father drives down the road to pick up fish and chips. If ever I have a craving for a meal from my childhood, I simply have to wait until the correct day of the week, then show up at my parents' front door. For years I thought of this as a burden.

Now, my mother's voice cuts through. Why don't you have a nap, Julia? We'll be alright here. I'll wake you if he starts fretting.

I realise I've been stood for a long time, staring blankly, not saying a word. I'm exhausted, it's true. But I know I won't be able to sleep. I have too much on my mind. Thanks, I say. It's fine, I'm fine. Really.

My mother looks at me. Her face is soft and pink, her eyes small and moist. She's looking at me differently, since the baby. Nobody tells you how hard it is, do they? she says. I think everyone's trying to forget.

I shake my head. I didn't really do anything, I say. It was all Nim.

My mother moves her gaze down to the baby. There's something on her face I haven't seen before, something like peace. You're a single mother to a newborn, she says. That means doing an awful lot, in my book.

I'm not his mother, I say.

My voice breaks on the last word, and I realise I'm crying. My mother settles the baby in his bouncer and comes to me, enveloping me in her fabric conditioner smell. Sweetheart, she says. Don't say that.

But I'm not.

Of course you are.

He knows I'm not. I can see it in his eyes.

My mother puts her hands on my shoulders and holds me at arm's length. Her look is stern. Hey, she says. This was never going to be easy, but you've waited years for this. Stop doubting it.

I sniff. Nim's gone, I say.

I know you were fond of her, sweetheart. But that was always the plan, wasn't it?

No. I mean she's *gone*. She's disappeared. The police are looking. She just walked out the hospital straight after the birth, didn't tell anyone where she was going. All her stuff's still here.

My mother doesn't speak for a while. Could she have gone to her parents'? she asks.

I shake my head. She'd never go there, I say.

Well, where was she planning to move to, once the baby arrived?

I shake my head again. I don't know, I whisper.

You must have had a plan, says my mother.

We did, but he came a month early, and we hadn't sorted anything out.

The baby starts to snuffle in his chair, and my mother lifts him out again. He's so small against her, I'd almost forgotten. I realise my father has gone silent in the kitchen, that in all likelihood he's been listening in this entire time. I know what they're both thinking, and it's that Nim's disappearance may mean she's having second thoughts about giving up the baby. I want to scream at them that the baby is not ours to keep, that he is a part of Nim, a physical part of her. It was only yesterday that I watched him emerge from her heaving, perfect body, that I saw the two of them split in half with my own eyes, and I came to understand, finally, that losing one of them is the same as losing both. By then, of course, it was too late.

14

For her first month working at the club, Nim came in every night we were open, sliced lime wedges and cracked lids from beer bottles without fault. She wore her tracksuits as if they were a uniform. She buzzed little lines into her eyebrows, into the hair behind her temples. She paid no attention at all to Leon, so that anyone looking on would never have guessed that they'd slept together. As well as this, the students barely seemed to notice her, outside of ordering drinks. She may have been the same age as them, but she dressed differently, and she talked differently too. It was perhaps for these reasons that she became a partner to me, behind the bar, in a way that no other of my employees had ever been. Nim was as hard-working as I was, as invisible. We went for breakfast at Buddie's five times in four weeks, and each time I bought her a fried egg sandwich and a cup of tea. I could tell she had no money, because she took every single shift I handed to her, and she never once called in sick. Over breakfast, I'd find myself confiding in her about Leon. I'd hardly talked to anyone about my marriage, neither at the time nor since. I was too proud. But Nim drew the truth out of me easily, with her intense eye contact and quick laugh. I found myself bringing up Leon of my own accord, found myself seeking out her opinion. It was addictive to talk about him, once I got going.

I told Nim about the time I'd revealed to a student who I knew was sleeping with Leon exactly what I thought of him. The girl was called Aaliyah. She'd worked at the club. She was studying history of art, had a blue afro washed out to the colour of seafoam. She wore a necklace with a pendant that disappeared into her cleavage. I'd seen her and Leon around the place, whispering in corners, kissing and holding hands. One night she and I were out back, loading rubbish bags into the huge wheelie bins. There was a fingernail moon, and I'd decided that if I didn't say it then, I never would.

Leon's a narcissist, I'd said. He's capable only of receiving. He won't give you a thing. I never wanted children, Aaliyah, and then I married one.

Aaliyah was stood with her fist tight around the plastic knot of the bin bag. She didn't speak for a moment, only blinked. I was proud of that speech, initially. It had come out of me fast, in a rush of air, and afterwards I felt lithe and easy, as if I'd been bloated for a long time. The part about not wanting children was a lie, of course, but I liked how it sounded. Aaliyah continued to stare at me, and then she frowned.

And yet you're still married to him? she said. That's kind of depressing.

Her pity had washed over me, slowly at first and then all at once. I bristled with shame. I'd made a fool of myself, when I'd intended to make a fool out of Leon.

Nim laughed through her nose, when I told her this story. How did that man get so jammy? she said.

That was why I liked talking to her about Leon. She saw the humour in it, the complete ridiculousness of my marriage. She didn't pity me, didn't speak of trauma, and I liked her for that. I laughed too, and the laughter was good. Leon was no more than a joke to us. It was wonderful.

D'you ever see yourself with anyone else? she asked me later, when we were walking home.

We'd worked out by then that her place was directly en route back to mine, so I'd drop her off there after Buddie's before carrying on up the hill. The lamp posts were spilling glow onto the pavements, and tiny flakes of snow were coming down, melting the moment they hit the tarmac. Christmas wasn't far off. Nim had tried to catch a few snowflakes on her tongue. I'd tried too, walking with my head tossed back and not looking where I was going, until I banged into a lamp post. Nim had laughed bent double, her big coat muffling the sound.

No way, I said, in answer to her question. I can't imagine ever being in love again. What about you?

I've been on a couple of dates since I got here, she said. Both through dating apps.

Do you like using apps? I asked.

No, she said. It's supposed to be easier, but I find it's so much more work. Someone will look cool online, then you meet and there's no chemistry. Other times I'll try and text for a while first, just to make sure we've got stuff in common, but then on the date I get worried I'm repeating myself, because I've forgotten who I've told what.

I don't think of you as scatty, I said.

Nim snorted. I'm not with you.

Why not?

I don't want to get fired.

I'd never fire you, Nim.

She smiled at me, her teeth glinting. Good, she said. Bar work suits my brain. I'd be a mess without it. I need something fast-paced and physical, otherwise I can't focus. I did shit in school, you know? I have, like, two GCSEs.

Seriously? But you're so smart.

That's what I said!

Nim blushed at that, and looked away from me. I loved her shy moments; they were like looking at her from a different angle.

There is this one person I like, said Nim. But she's pretty hard to read.

Oh yeah? Someone from the apps?

Nim waved her hand. I dunno, she said. Leave it. I don't wanna jinx it.

Fair enough, I said. I slept with Carlos recently. That's my only news.

Carlos, as in the bouncer?

Yeah. A few weeks back. The same night you slept with Leon.

Are you serious? You kept that quiet.

I shrugged. It wasn't a big deal. It hasn't happened since.

Was it good, at least?

Not really. Was Leon?

Ugh. He tried not to use a condom. Have I told you that?

I mean, I'm not surprised.

He got pissy when I told him to put one on. He must have been using some shitty brand, because it broke inside me.

Shit, Nim.

Don't worry. I got a morning-after. When I asked him to pay for it he tried to give me a gram of coke instead. He was so confused when I wouldn't just take the baggie. He didn't seem to get that I needed actual money, because I didn't have enough in my bank account to buy the pill otherwise.

We were outside Nim's by now, and she invited me up. I'd not been inside before.

We'll have to be pretty quiet, she said. But I've got a bottle of brandy under my bed. Come warm your insides, so you can make it home.

15

Nim's street was two blocks back from the seafront. It was lined with terraced houses, pebbledash pummelled by the wind. She turned her key in the lock. The hallway was lit with a bare bulb dangling from the ceiling, the walls half covered in floral wallpaper and half ripped away to reveal the plaster beneath. On the ceiling were great rings of greenish damp, the unmistakable smell of mould lingering in the air. I followed her up the narrow, creaky stairs. I'd thought living with Leon had been bad, but this place made his look cosy. It was as freezing inside as it was out. The house was narrow, with space for only a single room on each floor, but it stood tall, at four storeys high. The stairs seemed to go on forever, getting narrower and more rickety with each flight. I noticed black mould in the corners, creeping across the windowsills. Nim's bedroom was in the attic. The room was bare, also very cold, with no furniture but a single bed and a clothes rail, her hoodies thrown over the bar in the absence of hangers. There was a phone charger plugged into the far wall, a heated blanket which Nim switched on.

Where's all your stuff? I asked.

Nim shrugged. I left my mum's in a rush.

It was difficult being there, in the room where she lived. I had a horrible urge to cry, but I knew I couldn't do so in front of her. I'd understood already that Nim had no money, had noticed that she always wore the same few clothes, but I hadn't imagined anything close to this level of emptiness, to this sense of abandonment. The idea that she slept here every night pained me physically; there was a low ache in my heart.

What's he like, I asked, the landlord?

Oh, he's just some old boozer, she said. Hardly leaves his room, except to go to the pub. Sometimes I hear him ranting to himself, but he soon passes out.

She was crouched on the floor, reaching under her bed for the brandy. I hide it here, she explained, in case he tries to steal it.

It's just you and him living here?

Yep.

Nim, what if he's dangerous?

She stood up, unscrewed the bottle and took a swig. I reckon I could have him, she said. He's pretty unsteady on his feet. One good punch, he'd be down.

She passed me the bottle. I took a swig, and the burn was warming. You know I could lend you some money, I said. If you wanted a deposit for somewhere nicer. I could help.

Nim frowned. Jules, she said. I don't want your money. I'll work for it.

You already are working. It'll take you months to save enough to move.

She drank a little more brandy. Let's not do this now, she said. It's not nightcap talk.

Despite myself, I smiled. What is nightcap talk? I asked.

She looked off while she thought about it. I've been writing poems, she said.

Can I hear one?

No way.

Why not?

They're full of secrets.

Where d'you write them?

On the beach, usually. I'd never seen the sea in my life, before I came here. Now I swim every day.

You're joking. It's December.

She shrugged. I started when I first arrived, in late summer, and I kept up the habit.

You're lying.

She scowled. Don't say that.

I apologised, swallowed back the panic in my throat. Nim was like that, always on the edge of a new mood. Now, she appeared to accept my sorry easily. Come in with me, she said.

Give it six months, then maybe.

I'm going in on Christmas Day. I heard people do that here, there's some tradition.

You'll be here for Christmas?

Where else would I be?

I nodded, knowing better than to bring up her family. I'll watch you swim on Christmas Day, I said. I won't come in, but I'll watch.

She raised the bottle in the air, pleased, then took another slug. See? she said. Now this is nightcap talk.

I left quite soon after that. It was almost seven o'clock in the morning; the sun had risen but the moon was still up in the solid blue sky. Everything was crisp and white with frost, and the grass on the green outside my block crunched as I walked across it. The cold rushed in through the seams of my coat, and when I got inside there was a searing sensation in the ends of my fingers as they thawed out.

I pressed the button for the lift. Riding upwards, I thought of Nim in her tiny dank room, swilling a bottle of brandy. Then I imagined Leon there too. I'd been good at avoiding thinking of the night they spent together, but since Nim had told me about the condom, since I'd seen the place where it had happened, I'd felt the vision sketching itself slowly in the edges of my mind. Now I was alone, I couldn't keep myself from looking. I pictured his scrawny hands on her, the oily hair on his blue-white chest, his Adam's apple pressing like a thumb into her neck. The knowledge that Leon had been inside Nim made me sick. I could feel the bile rising, acrid, in the pipe of my neck. In my flat, I tried to sleep, and couldn't.

16

We held our final night of the year on the twentieth of the month, the same day that term ended at the university. Leon arrived in a felt Santa suit and a pair of red high-top trainers, a hessian sack slung over his shoulder. Inside the sack were bottles of Sourz, flavoured either green apple or red cherry, for the colour scheme. He stood in the middle of the dance floor all night handing out free shots, just as he did every year. Leon wasn't one for effort, usually, but Christmas was his holiday of choice. Each year, his mother sent him a hamper filled with bottles of champagne, candy canes, and a kit to build your own gingerbread house. I always thought this was extreme behaviour, vaguely American. Leon would eat the slabs of gingerbread straight from the box, squirt the icing into the back of his mouth. Not once, for as long as we were married, did the house get built.

That night Leon was bright-eyed, manic with festivity. He'd waltzed over to the bar when we'd first opened, given me a slow pirouette. How'd I look? he'd asked.

Gaunt, I'd replied flatly. Positively malnourished.

Leon had hitched up his trousers, visibly hurt, rejigged the hessian sack on his shoulder and turned back into the crowd. That was our dynamic: he was stupid and spoiled; I was cold. I suspected that he hoped for friendship, for something sibling-adjacent, but I withheld any glimmer of fondness I felt towards him. I intended to punish him forever. That was my job, surely, as his ex-wife. He was a dickhead, and he'd never learn. Still, as he walked back into the dance floor, I remembered the first year we spent Christmas together, when he'd given me a bike that he'd bought off Gumtree and spray-painted silver. There was a half-rotten basket on it, attached with cable ties. The bike would hardly even ride. Later I paid two hundred pounds at the cycle shop to have everything but the frame replaced. The shopkeeper had advised me to just buy a new one, but I'd refused. That summer – the first summer we were married – Leon and I cycled all over the city, a baguette sticking up out my basket. We could have been in Paris, if it wasn't for all the Tescos.

That night in the club, the students necked Leon's free shots, and Nim and I sold almost no drinks as a result. At the end of the night, the DJ put on 'Last Christmas' and the whole club belted the lyrics upwards into the thick cloud of skunk that hung over the dance floor, weaker streams of bubblegum vape caught between. Nim and I joined in the singalong from behind the bar. I was wearing a length of tinsel that a student had given Nim, and which Nim had wrapped around my neck like a scarf. She and I were each drinking a Baby Guinness. At the chorus, Nim took my hands and held them to her chest as she serenaded me. I laughed. It was the closest I'd ever been to carolling.

I didn't see Nim again until Christmas Day, when I met her at ten o'clock in the morning on the beach for her swim. I brought mulled wine in a flask and slices of shop-bought fruit cake individually wrapped in plastic. There was a small crowd on the beach when I arrived, stripped down to their costumes. One old, leathery man had brought a jar of goose fat and was covering himself in it. Nim's cheeks were pink with cold, mottled like a rash. She was wearing her grey hoodie under her big coat, the cord pulled tight and tied in a bow, so that her ears and head were hidden. I felt slightly delirious at the sight of her. Christmas was a day mostly reserved for my parents, for their dreary rituals. Now, Nim ate her fruit cake in three bites and took a long slug of wine, though I had intended for both things to be for after her swim. I grinned; her impatience made me merry. She was jigging up and down on the spot, and she admitted to me that she was nervous about getting in the water. It was especially cold that morning.

You don't have to do it, I said.

But you've come all the way here.

All the way here? It's a ten-minute walk.

She blew some air through her lips, vibrating them. Her breath smelled like marzipan. Jeez, she said. You really know how to make a girl feel special.

My ears went hot. Nim looked at me out of the corner of her eye. She understood exactly how to make me flustered, and she could do it very easily. She unzipped her coat and pulled her hoodie over her head, followed by her big red T-shirt. She was wearing a black swimming costume under tracksuit bottoms, white stripes down the sides of her ribs. She wriggled out of her trousers, already shuddering at the chill, and then she shook her feet through the leg holes without removing her trainers. Her body was lean but not skinny; the flesh on her thighs rocked as she jogged down the hill of pebbles towards the sea. She was long and awkward, both unfinished and splendid at the same time, like a sapling. The crunch-ing sound made by her feet faded as she moved further away. A few metres before the shore she kicked her shoes off and stuffed her socks inside them. The sun shone weak, giving the light a washed-out quality. She slowed again when she hit the water, transferring from a gallop to a wade, pushed forward by nothing but her own rhythm. When she was deep enough, she hurled herself in. She swam toward the horizon, brisk, trying to regain some inner warmth. There were four or five other people in the water with her, panting in their bobble hats. Nim stood out easily, her shaved head smooth and dark against the flat, grey sea. She was the only swimmer brave enough to dip fully under. I sat on the pebbles with my legs pulled in, my chin resting on my knees.

After, her lips were blue. Her hair was so wet it appeared webbed, like an otter's. She wrapped herself in a pink towel and jumped up and down on the pebbles for a while, sea water weaving through the hair on her legs. She picked up my slice of fruit cake and ate it without asking. Someone had brought a kettle on a gas burner, and they gave her tea in a tin mug. The steam coming out of the kettle looked solid in the low light. I asked Nim if she wanted to come to my parents' house for lunch, and she shook her head.

They'll think I'm some kind of stray, she said.

Oh please, I said. The last person I brought home for Christmas was Leon.

Nim laughed. Right, she said. The bar's so low it's in hell.

Is that a yes?

She sniffed, swallowed the dregs of her tea. I guess, she said.

We walked to Portslade from the beach. The journey took almost an hour, along the coast then up through Hove. I talked more than Nim did. I told her about the one Christmas I spent with Leon and his mother at my parents' house, how Rita had worn a white silk dress with a feather collar and chained-smoked inside the house all day, to which my parents had been too polite to say anything. She'd given my father a coffee table book of *Playboy* centrefolds, and he'd been so shocked upon opening it that he'd dropped it on his big toe, leaving him unable to walk for a week. Cooped up in the living room to keep my father company, his foot propped beneath a bag of frozen peas, we'd all got too drunk, Leon the worst. He'd told inappropriate story after inappropriate story, to which I had blushed and sweated while Rita laughed with her head tipped back, so that her paper crown slid off. I could see all the fillings in her molars, her tongue stained black with wine, and it was the only time I'd ever seen her look ugly.

Christmas with Nim was not nearly so eventful. She was quiet at my parents' house, fastidiously polite, constantly offering to fill glasses or help my mother with the food. She evaded questions about her personal life, answering anything my parents asked her with another question directed at them, or else a compliment about the warmth of the house, the tastiness of the meal. She ate an incredible amount, accepting everything that was offered to her, but not before checking each time if my parents were sure there was really enough. Nim kept her mouth permanently full, I thought, so that she could avoid talking. That, or she was just filling up for free while she had the chance.

After pudding, we took our places in the living room – Nim and I on the squashy sofa, my parents on their armchairs – and exchanged a few small presents. There was nothing for Nim, since none of us had known that she was coming, and I expected nothing from her. I was surprised, then, when she reached into her pockets and pulled out three pebbles. There was one with a hole straight through for my mother, one slashed with a perfect line of pure white for my father, and for me, a skimming stone, blue-black and large enough to fill my palm.

Where did you get these? I asked. You can't have picked them all out on the beach just now. I'd have seen you.

I've been collecting them since I moved here, she said. I carry them around with me. I don't know why, really. For times like this, I guess.

Nim was stood in the middle of my parents' sitting room, having got up to hand the pebbles out, wearing her big tracksuit. Her shaved head was frosted with dried salt, her smile bashful, her eyes on the carpet. There followed a short moment of quiet, in which my parents — two people who had never before paid any attention to a pebble — turned their gifts over in their hands. I remember thinking, in that quiet, how bizarre Nim was, in her way, and how enchanting. She was not capable, however hard she tried, however shy she felt, of hiding this, at least not for any substantial period of time. My parents thanked Nim. They placed their pebbles on the mantlepiece. I slipped mine into my pocket. My mother switched the television on and brought a tub of Quality Street through to the sofa, to signify that we were at last done socialising. Nim ate six chocolates in quick succession, then fell immediately to sleep. Her snore was nasal, the irregular wheeze of a pet.

17

The club didn't open again until a week into January, when the new term started. I saw Nim only once before then, when she called me and asked if I wanted to go to the pier.

To bring the year in, she said.

Nim, it's the fourth already.

Close enough, isn't it?

I met her by the doughnuts, in the driving rain. She was sheltering under a striped awning, her face pressed up to the glass, watching the greasy machine ferry rounds of batter into a vat of hot oil. I shuffled in next to her, dripping. Hey, I said.

This would be a sick job, she said. Look, he hardly has to do anything, and the smell is so good.

The man working the kiosk stuck a pair of metal tongs into the oil and flipped the doughnuts over, revealing their dark gold undersides. I don't know, I said. The splashback off that vat must be lethal.

Nim and I still hadn't made eye contact, both of us stood with our noses to the glass. Her breath clouded her vision, and she lifted a gloved hand to wipe the mist away. The tongs came back, and the gently bobbing doughnuts were lifted out of the oil, rolled through a tray of granulated sugar and tossed into a paper bag. The bag was passed through the window to Nim, dark spots of grease already growing on the paper.

Watch out, I said. She's after your job.

I don't know why I said that; I was giddy that day. I wasn't worried about Nim quitting the club for the doughnut kiosk. She would get bored here, I knew. She relied on stimulation in order to focus, and being good at her work meant something to her. Then again, her life would be easier at the kiosk, the hours far more reasonable and the money most likely the same. The club paid Nim minimum wage, just as any other starter job in hospitality would have. It was barely enough to live on, I understood, Brighton these days being almost as expensive as London. In my lifetime, the city had morphed from a seaside town into something like a suburb of the capital, populated each year by a larger and larger number of commuters. They came here for the sea air, for the novelty of street stalls selling tie-dye dresses and rings bent from old silver spoons, and they made it unliveable.

The man in the kiosk blinked. His glasses were steamed over. We need someone for the weekends, he said.

Nim threaded her arm through mine, an offer of reassurance, and clamped down tight. She paid in cash for the doughnuts, immediately burned her tongue and swore about it. The rain was lashing down. All the other kiosks were closed.

You picked a good day for the pier, I said.

Doughnut steam escaped Nim's mouth like cigarette smoke. The burn hadn't seemed to put her off. We made it halfway down the pier, then took shelter in the arcade. We played the coin slots for a while. The sugar from the doughnuts felt like sand on my lips. I bought us two rounds on the dance machine, where someone had left four empty cans of Special Brew lined up on top of the box. I scored higher than Nim and took my win seriously, since she was young and I wasn't. My hair was wet, and every time I'd stamped my foot a few drops had sprayed off and landed on Nim's face. Afterwards, as we were leaving the arcade, she blamed those drops for the fact she hadn't won.

I was basically in the shower, she said. It was distracting. You should shave your head, like me. Then we can have a fair match.

Right, I said. It's my hair that's the problem, not your two left feet.

Nim stopped still in the middle of the rain and stood with her mouth hung open, playing at being offended. After that, we gave up hope of not getting soaked. The rain worked its way through each layer of my clothes. I could feel my feet wrinkling up inside my shoes. I don't know what had come over me and Nim that day. We were acting drunk, I swear. We kept bumping hips while we walked, laughing ourselves into hysterics. I can't remember what she was saying that was so funny. All of the rides on the pier were closed because of the rain, but we managed to sneak onto the trampolines and bounce around for a while. There was a small puddle in the middle of each, water not yet seeped through the mesh, and when we bounced the puddles rushed up and sprayed into the air all around us, making more rain. The black squares of stretchy floor gleamed. There were funhouse mirrors lining the pen, scratched up so badly that we saw no detail in our reflections.

We got kicked off the trampolines eventually, by a middle-aged woman with a big umbrella and a hi-vis. On your way kids, she shouted. You've had your fun.

We scarpered before she could try to charge us anything, and by the time we reached the end of the pier the rain was lighter. We lingered for a while, looking through the gaps in the wood floor, some wide enough to slip a whole hand through, down to the sea below, the cast-iron beams that held us up. Seagulls waiting in the beams began to ruffle their feathers for flight, now that the rain was finally easing. One by one they dropped down into the air and wheeled out from under us, into the open sky. I followed a seagull with my eyes and found that the sun had dipped and the light was going, a haze of yellow-pink coming up off the horizon.

Nim, I said. Look.

A rounded black shape was humming in the low sky. It stretched out long, then disappeared as the angle changed. What the fuck? said Nim.

The shape came back, a near-perfect oval, scattered at the edges. They're starlings, I said. You've never seen that?

Never, said Nim.

There'll be more soon, I said.

We waited, and more came. Clean shapes grew together and split apart, like bubbles in a lava lamp. I must have seen this spectacle fifty times, and still it amazed me. Nim looked on in silence, a slight frown on her face that gradually softened. When she noticed I was watching her, she got self-conscious and cast her eyes down. That's deep, she said.

We went for a pint in the pub. There was an open fire, and we sat at the closest table to it and took our shoes off. My feet looked awful, the skin wadded and soft. My phone had got wet in my pocket, and Nim asked the kitchen for a bowl of uncooked rice to put it in, padding over to the bar in her bare feet. She told me she'd come to this pub on New Year's Eve, and at midnight she'd kissed a woman who'd had her tongue surgically split so that it forked like a snake's.

Christ, I said. Did it look good?

Not really, said Nim. But that's what I liked about her. She didn't care.

Hey, I said. How's your crush?

Nim took a long pull on her beer. What crush?

The one you told me about, I said. The one who's hard to read.

Oh that, said Nim. That's the same.

The same?

She lifted her pint to the light and narrowed her eyes at it. Is your drink alright? she asked. Mine tastes weird.

I cocked my head, sensing she was trying to change the subject. I sipped my beer. Mine's normal, I said.

I passed my glass to Nim, so she could see for herself. She drank it and shivered. Ugh, she said. Yours is even worse.

Lightweight, I said.

She gave the rest of her beer to me, and I moved onto it after my own. Nim ate a bowl of dry-roasted peanuts instead, throwing them into the air and catching them with her mouth. We stayed long enough for our socks to dry. When I put mine on, they were crunchy and smelled like barbeque. After that, Nim and I went our separate ways. It was just past four o'clock, but it felt like midnight.

18

I didn't think about Nim's rejection of her pint until a month later, when she told me she was pregnant. She was in my flat, sitting on the sofa, chewing at her hang-nails. It was three o'clock in the afternoon. I'd made coffee, which she hadn't touched.

It was in the pub that it dawned on me, she said. Remember I couldn't drink that beer?

I nodded. My mouth was dry.

I realised I couldn't remember the last time I'd had a period, said Nim. That night, I went home and took a test.

I thought of her catching peanuts in her mouth, the fire going, all the while her wondering if she could be pregnant. You've known that long? I said. That was weeks ago. I've had you work so many long nights since then.

I called the clinic the next day, said Nim. I've been waiting for a surgical abortion. I didn't want to do an at-home one, with my drunk landlord raging down-stairs, and it's taken ages to get the appointment.

I shook my head. You should have told me, I said. You could have done it here.

I'm telling you now, Jules.

It's true I was offended that she'd been keeping the secret from me, as self-indulgent as that was. I worried it meant something about our friendship, the fact she hadn't felt able to come to me straight away. Then it hit me, the reason why. It's Leon's, I said.

Her nod was so small it was almost imperceptible. I guess the morning-after pill failed, she said. I've heard that can happen.

I blew some air out my cheeks, vibrating my lips like a motorbike. I asked her when her appointment was.

Tomorrow, she said.

What time?

Ten o'clock.

I'll come with you.

It's—

You can come back here after, I said. You can stay as long as you need. I won't have you back at work until you're fully recovered, Nim, so don't even try.

Jules.

I looked at her.

I've been thinking, she said. You want a baby, right?

I blinked. That question seemed to have come out of nowhere. I didn't understand, initially, what she meant. Very slowly I gauged her meaning. Oh Nim, I said. I'd been standing to talk to her, but now I edged towards to the sofa and sat down.

I couldn't do that, I said.

Why not?

I raked a hand through my hair. It wouldn't be right, I said. I don't know if it would be legal, even.

Nim shrugged. I don't really care what's legal, she said. This is my baby, I can do what I want.

I only stared at her. She was completely serious. Stop looking at me like that, she said. I'm not pro-life or anything. I just think: you want a baby and I've got one. It makes sense.

I shook my head. It makes no sense at all, I said.

I should never have slept with Leon, Jules. It was a stupid mistake. But we can reverse it. We can make it right.

You don't have to do that, Nim. It doesn't matter.

Of course it matters, she said. Her eyes were shiny, and she scrubbed them with the heel of her hand. Raise this baby, she said. I want you to.

I can't, I whispered. Thank you, Nim, but I just can't.

Why? she demanded. You haven't given me a good enough reason.

I sighed. I think you're underestimating it, I said. You can't carry a baby, give birth to it and then just hand it over.

Sure I can. Other people do. Surrogacy, adoption. These things happen all the time.

You're being naïve.

She bristled at that. Don't treat me like a child, she said.

I shook my head. I just don't understand why you'd want to do this.

Nim gave me a long, even look. Her brow had softened, but her gaze was severe. I like you, Jules, she said. I care about you. I want you to have what you want. Is that not enough?

I put my hand to my forehead and smoothed the skin there. Her generosity unnerved me. It wasn't enough. I wanted her to want something from me in return. I'll pay you, I said.

She started to laugh. Tell me you're joking, she said.

I folded my arms across my chest, defensive.

Nim chewed her lip. I've been thinking this over for weeks, Jules. That's why I didn't tell you sooner. I wanted to be certain.

I shook my head, but the shake was weaker than before. I could already feel my resistance dying out. Think about it, she said. Take some time.

We don't have time, Nim. Your abortion is tomorrow.

She stood then, started to pull on her jacket. I looked at her body, hidden as usual beneath her baggy clothes, searching for signs of growth that I knew wouldn't yet have appeared. I'll see you at the club, she said.

No you won't, I said. I'll have someone cover for you.

She looked like she was about to protest, but changed her mind. Perhaps she chose to let me win this small battle, so that she might win the much larger one. Call me in the morning, she said.

I listened as the front door clicked closed, as the lift chimed and lowered. I turned Nim's idea over and over in my mind, until things were spinning so fast I could hardly see, let alone think. I closed my eyes, and I couldn't help but imagine the baby. It wasn't an image that came to me, particularly, but a sensation. The sensation was of steadiness, of warmth, like a cat's weight in my lap. Slowly my mind calmed, the whirling slowed to a lull.

Did I know even then that I would accept? Perhaps, though really I think it took some hours more. It took my shift in the club that night, working alone in the sweat-filled dark, watching Leon lift a key to his nose in the puffed haze of a fog machine. It took my fleeting panic that he would be a useless father, immediately replaced by the understanding that I had known this for all the years that we were married, and it had not once stopped

me from hoping to get pregnant by him. I wasn't troubled by the idea of being a single mother; if anything I
preferred it. I was a control freak, and I thrived when
I was in charge. I was better company one-on-one, and
found managing multiple relationships at the same time
complicated. Besides, my full set of parents hadn't given
me a feeling of solidity growing up, but rather of claus-
trophobia. I felt sure that having one parent was enough.

At the end of the night I locked up, walked home,
slept for four hours, and then woke to an alarm and
called Nim, my voice still groggy with sleep. I'll do it,
I said.

You will?

Yes.

I'll call the clinic now, she said. I'll cancel.

Nim?

Mm.

Will you move in here for the pregnancy?

I didn't know that I was going to say that, until I
did. I had thought it over, albeit briefly, but I hadn't
intended to ask so soon. There was a pause.

You don't have to, I said. I just thought you might be
more comfortable, and you could save money on rent.

I'd like that, she said.

Oh, I said. OK. OK, good. Whenever you want, then.

Jules?

Yeah.

I'm happy. Just so you know. About the baby, I mean. I think this is right.

My eyes prickled. For a moment I couldn't speak, I couldn't muster the words. My life had been small and dark for so long, and now Nim had prised her way inside and detonated it. All around me were smithereens. I looked up, and found scraps of sky.

19

Nim moved in almost immediately, carrying nothing but a backpack. I'd made no preparations for her, either spatially or emotionally. In fact, I'd vastly underestimated how different my life would become once we lived together. Her move had been decided within the rush of my decision to raise her baby, a decision so huge that it cast everything else into shadow. I welcomed her timidly, with a chocolate biscuit and the insistence that she take my bed. For almost a month I slept on the sofa, overheating inside a nylon sleeping bag, my hips sore in the mornings and my neck full of cricks. We ate various soups that I cooked from scratch and served with garlic bread dug from the supermarket deep freeze.

When Nim caught me on my laptop, looking into buying a futon for the floor, she suggested that we share the bed. I'd tried to refuse, conscious of overcrowding her in her condition, but she'd insisted.

It's a waste to buy something just for these months, she said. You can spend that money on the baby. Anyway, there's room in the bed.

It was Nim's plan, right from the beginning, to move out as soon as the baby was born. I had offered to set her up in a flat, paying the first few months' worth of rent, so that she'd have somewhere to recover after the labour. She hadn't yet agreed to this, resistant as she was to handouts, but in my mind it was the obvious arrangement.

The first night Nim and I shared a bed she slept heavily, barely moving at all, her breathing very deep. I struggled to get comfortable next to her, resisting my urge to toss and turn, which only made me more conscious of the fact I couldn't sleep. I hadn't shared a bed regularly since Leon, and I wasn't used to it. In the morning, Nim rose early and I slept on. When I got up, she was sitting on the sofa, eating toast.

You're never up before me, I said.

I know, she said. I slept great. Better than I have in months, actually. Did you sleep well?

Yeah, I lied. Fine.

From then on we continued to share. Over the weeks, I got used to having her there, and soon I was sleeping normally. It was funny, climbing in together at night, me reaching over to flick the lamp off. Sometimes one of us would giggle, at the strangeness of it more than anything, at how close we were to a pregnant hetero-sexual couple, and at the same time how far. We'd laugh together for a bit, both lying down so that the giggles came too easily, started to hurt. Eventually they'd peter out into silence, into sleep.

It was around this time that I reduced Nim's hours at the club, though I paid her the same. I would have had her not working at all, but she refused, saying she'd be bored without the shifts. Behind the bar, she was as proficient as ever, radiating her same offbeat charm. Her preg-nancy remained a secret between the two of us, hinted at when I rushed to stop her lifting a heavy crate, or when I pressed her to go home early. We cradled the fact of her pregnancy between us, shuffling about with it like two penguins with an egg.

Though I tried to look after Nim at home, she did not take well to it. I filled the fridge and cupboards with nutritious snacks, following recipes that I found online for superfood muffins or energy balls, but still I regularly came home to find her boiling Super Noodles on the hob.

When she first moved in I did all of her washing, hanging her tracksuits to dry over the radiators, over the backs of the doors, but she told me off for this, saying she didn't like her things too clean. It came to a head one morning when we needed milk. She offered to go out to buy some, and I tried to give her the money. She'd rolled her eyes at me, dropped my coins onto the kitchen counter and stormed out. When she came back she'd bought more milk than we needed, just to prove a point, and I took to making porridge in the mornings to use it up. I could see by then that I was irritating her, that though I should have learned from my parents not to smother people, I had not. I apologised to Nim for this, over the porridge.

Sometimes I worry it's impossible not to turn into our parents, I said.

Ugh, said Nim. Don't say shit like that.

She hadn't told me much about her family, only dropped small hints like these, hints which I remained too afraid to pick up and ask her about. She could be so cutting, when she chose to be; she could crush me with a sneer of her lip, a knit of her brow.

I'm not looking after you because I don't think you're capable of doing it yourself, I said to her. It's because you're giving me a baby, Nim. I know nothing I do could possibly equal this, but you could at least let me try.

She grimaced. This isn't a trade, she said. I'm not swapping you a child for free milk and half a bed.

I'm *giving* you a child because I'm really fucking self-less, OK?

Nim was good at that, when she was in the right mood: turning any spat into a joke. Still, she would not back down, not ever.

Outside of these initial power struggles, living with Nim was a comfort. We watched crap television, we took walks along the seafront, we drank mug after mug of tea. Nim kept up her swimming, and often I'd go along to watch. When I worked a shift without Nim, I found that the simple act of telling her about it the following morning ridded me of the irritations involved. Leon would be useless, Carlos would be overly sincere, the students would be demanding, but still I could go home to Nim and find that none of it really mattered. Her company soothed me, and the baby inside her gave me perspective.

There were gestures, too, moments our living together felt almost romantic. Like on Valentine's Day, when the gravel in the smoking area became filled with cigarette butts stained red and pink and maroon with lipstick, and I returned home at five-thirty in the morning to find a jam jar of water on the kitchen counter, in it a single rose. Or when I was ill with a cold and Nim made me a hot water bottle, tucked it under the duvet while I was sleeping. I thought we were being funny, I thought we were laughing at ourselves. For being so close to a couple, but not. She would have the baby, and then she would leave. That was the big twist. What could you do but laugh?

I remained convinced that I wasn't drawn to her romantically. She could make me nervous, sure, she could make me blush, but that was because I thought highly of her, and because I found her impossible to figure out. She had a past packed with secrets, a new life blooming in her womb. Her strength intimidated me, her generosity even more. Though I found her beautiful – always I found her beautiful – I wouldn't have considered kissing her. She was eighteen years old, she was a child, and though she never would've admitted it, she was vulnerable. She was pregnant and penniless, with no family support. If she'd been ten years older, I thought, maybe. If I'd ever considered myself attracted to women, maybe. But neither of these things were true. She was a friend to me, and she was one of the best friends I'd ever had.

Perhaps my favourite part of her pregnancy, looking back, were those early days, when nobody knew but us, when there were no complicated questions to answer, no judgement from the outside. The flat became a kind of womb, in its way, windows misty against the winter, the heating cranked up because I was worried about Nim getting cold, everybody on the outside only half visible, the walls of the flat working like a membrane.

Nim's belly didn't begin to noticeably protrude until she was four or five months along, and though I loved seeing her body change its contours, though her physical transformation captivated me, it's true that before her pregnancy began to show we were at our happiest. Back then, the baby had seemed so far off that there were moments when I wondered if Nim and I were making him up, indulging each other in some mad and beautiful fantasy. Some days, this was preferable to the bittersweet reality of the birth, at which point I would get my baby, but Nim would be gone. The closer we came to her due date, the closer we came to our separation.

20

Spring rolled around, weeds grew out of the cracks in the paving stones, and by late March there was no hiding Nim's pregnancy. She walked all over the city with her hoodie unzipped, her rounding belly peeking out over her waistband. She swam in the sea in her same costume, filling it out more and more each day, so the racing stripes began to gently bend. There was one night when Nim came to the club for work wearing that costume as a top, paired with her tracksuit bottoms, and an especially perceptive student noticed the slight curve of her belly and shouted her congratulations over the bar. I knew then that I would have to tell Leon, before he found out from somebody else. I knew also that once I told Leon, it would quickly become common knowledge in the club. He wasn't opposed to airing his dirty laundry in the smoking area; if anything he got off on it. He'd take any pity, any disgust, so long as his name was on another's lips.

I showed up at Leon's flat without warning. He hardly ever picked up the phone; there was almost no point in calling beforehand. I walked over in the early afternoon, under a warming sun, and there was blossom on the trees. He answered the buzzer after I'd pressed it five times then held it down hard for close to a minute. I could tell by his voice through the intercom that he'd been asleep. Inside, the smell of cigarettes made the air stale, and the walls were yellow from smoke. I cracked open a window and shoved a nest of clothes and sleeveless records from the sofa onto the floor, so that we could sit. The flat leather cushions were covered in little hairs of tobacco, which I brushed off with the flat of my palm. I hadn't visited in years, and already I could feel myself retracting to the person I'd been when we were still married, wound tight and jaded.

Leon, I called. Where are you?

He'd buzzed me in, left the front door on the latch and disappeared back into the bedroom before I'd walked inside. I'd assumed he was getting dressed, but now I wondered if he'd gone straight back to bed. Leon? I shouted again.

Finally he staggered into the room, pushing his untidy hair from his face with a clawed hand. There was a gaping hole in his T-shirt, revealing a semicircle of blue skin, sporadic dark hairs creeping up his belly. A cigarette dangled, like always, from his chapped lips. He smirked at me.

Look, I said. I've got something to tell you.

He slumped next to me on the sofa, a smile still playing at his mouth. Sounds ominous, he said.

It was like stepping back in time, all of it. I couldn't count the number of occasions on which I'd sat Leon down, on this very sofa, to confront him about another woman, about a sum of money he'd taken from the club's bank account that had meant our staff's wages had bounced, only to have him laugh and look at me like I had no sense of humour at all. It was here that I'd told him I was leaving him, that I'd found a flat and was filing for a divorce. I remember that he'd snorted at the news, initially, and then cried when it dawned on him that I was serious. I'd put a hand on his shoulder to comfort him, then snatched it away again, angry with myself. There'd been another time, two or three years before, when I'd broached an open marriage in an effort to save myself the humiliation of his affairs.

But we can't be open, he'd said. I'd be jealous.

He'd looked at me like I was very cruel, like his feelings meant nothing to me. What if you fall for someone else? he'd whispered.

What if *you* do? I'd replied. You've cheated on me constantly, Leon.

He'd only sniggered, shaken his head. He had a way of spinning his affairs to make out that he was merely a silly boy, that he fell into bed with the students entirely by accident, high or drunk, and that by making a big deal of it, by accusing him not only of infidelity but also of exploitation, I was being unreasonable. So many of our fights over his cheating had ended in me screaming at him in frustration while he either looked on, amused at my overreaction, or else sobbed and accused me of bullying. It was the same narrative when I divorced him. He wouldn't accept that he'd driven me to it. Rather I was abandoning him, I was seeing him only for his faults, I was making a drama out of nothing. After the divorce he fully shrank back from the running of the club, leaving all the work to me, claiming he was too depressed to help. I got a call from Rita the day I moved out of Leon's flat, in which she berated me for half an hour for the distress I'd caused her son.

Darling, she'd said. He hasn't asked me to talk to you, but I can't stand back and allow you to treat him like this. Upping and leaving without even a warning! You of all people should know how fragile he is. Have you forgotten he has a health condition?

I wanted to tell her that if she was so worried about Leon's heart, she should probably have a word with him about his cocaine habit, but I only bit my tongue and left my phone on loudspeaker while I unpacked a box of crockery.

I was expecting something similar from Leon in response when I told him about Nim. I was expecting an attempt to laugh it off, followed by genuine self-pity, a few tears. I was expecting a call from his mother, some weeks down the line, in order to fight his battle for him. Instead, he was monosyllabic, near impossible to read. I told him that Nim was pregnant, that the baby was his, that she had asked me to raise it and I had agreed. I kept my eyes on Leon as I spoke, searching his face for a reaction. For a long time, nothing came. He took in the information with a sneer on his face, looking not at me but at the far wall slightly to my right. He sat hunched into himself, no longer sprawled across the sofa but tense, jogging his foot incessantly.

Leon? I said.

Yeah.

Are you hearing this?

Yeah.

The baby will live with me, I said. I'll raise them as my own. But when they're old enough to process it, I don't intend to lie. I'll tell them about you, and about Nim. Does this sound alright to you? If you'd like to be more involved, we can talk about that.

Leon finished his cigarette and immediately rolled another. No, he said, without looking at me.

No?

I don't want to be involved. I don't want the kid to know about me at all.

I closed my eyes for a moment, took a breath. I understood that it would be easier not to have to deal with Leon as a parent, with his flaky and irresponsible behaviour. Still, I was taken aback by his briskness. On behalf on the baby, I was hurt.

You can mull it over, I said. We've got years before these questions come up.

I don't need to mull it over, Jules.

Well, Brighton's a pretty small city. You'll probably bump into us on the street, and that's not even mentioning the club.

You'll have to leave the club.

I gave a slow nod. If that's what you want, I said. I think you're being hasty, though. I know this isn't conventional, but—

The club belongs to me, remember?

I licked my lips. Well, who's going to run it? I asked.

I will.

You can't run it alone, Leon. You're not capable.

Not capable of running the club, not capable of being a father. Cheers, Jules. I appreciate that.

He spoke those words in a mumble. After, his eyes shifted back to the wall again, and I could tell that he was gone from me. I'd never seen him so removed. I wanted to shake him. Are you on something? I whispered.

No, Jules. For fuck's sake.

OK, OK. I'm sorry.

He tensed his jaw, so it flashed even more angular than usual. He looked old and ropey, bags smudged under his eyes. Congratulations, he said. Is that what I'm supposed to say?

I sniffed. Only if you mean it, I said.

He still wasn't looking at me. Well, he said. I know you always wanted a kid.

I frowned at him. Did you really? Why did you never mention it?

I thought it was my fault, he said. I thought I was shooting blanks. I didn't want to give you another excuse to leave me.

It was always impossible, with Leon, to construe whether he was being honest or playing the victim. This time, I gave him the benefit of the doubt. It wasn't your fault, I said. We know that for sure, now you've got someone else pregnant. It was mine.

At least one thing was, he whispered. He sniffed and looked at me. His eyes were like overboiled eggs: yellow irises, a ring of grey before the white. I hate myself even more than you hate me, he said, if that helps.

That doesn't help at all, Leon. Jesus.

When we were married, I'd downloaded an app on my phone to track my ovulation, but I never told Leon about it. I'd padded into the bathroom after sex and done shoulder stands against the cold tiled walls. We didn't speak explicitly about having a baby, though I dropped hints. I told his mother how much I loved children. I warned Leon I wasn't on contraception, and took the fact that he never used a condom as confirmation that he was open to the idea of becoming a parent. He rarely, if ever, used contraception with anyone, was the truth, and it had nothing to do with his plans for fatherhood. When we were married, he gave me chlamydia on three separate occasions.

Because we'd never properly discussed having a baby, we never acknowledged, either, the fact that I wasn't getting pregnant. He didn't bring it up with me, and at the time I assumed this was partly because he wasn't thinking much about it, and partly because I took such effort to hide my desperation from him. Now, I saw that my effort had not been entirely successful. Some amount of my desire had crept through. Why had I felt such need to hide it in the first place? Because I thought it made me needy, and I thought neediness made me ugly. It was always Leon who cried when I confronted him about his affairs; not once had I shed a tear.

My mother had never discussed her own struggles to conceive, nor her miscarriages, with me. I still remember very clearly my being told that I was going to be a big sister, rushing to school and telling everyone there. The news had given me a confidence that was uncommon in my childhood self. I got home that afternoon to find that my mother had gone to bed at four o'clock, and that there was a strange smell in the air outside the bathroom, like coins. My father and I had sandwiches for dinner, and I brushed my teeth at the kitchen sink. Nobody said a word about the baby, but I knew. The next morning my mother was up and about, but only just. Her face had a washed-out look, almost translucent, as if I could pass my hand straight through. A week later, when my classmates asked what month my baby sibling was coming, I told them I'd been lying. I said it without looking up from my lunch, and afterwards I could feel my classmates exchanging glances, having been reminded yet again that I was a freak and a loser, that it was exactly this kind of odd behaviour that was the reason I was always lumbered with the little kids in the playground, rather than friends my own age.

On the sofa with Leon, I watched as he ripped a flake of dry skin from his lip with his teeth and ate it. He was right. I had always wanted a baby, and for years I had wanted not just any baby, but his. I had prayed for it. Now, here we were. Something had gone very wrong for a long time, and at last it had come right. I believed that, then.

We'll always be in each other's lives, Leon. You know that?

He shrugged again. Stuck with me, he said.

I gave a small smile. I felt sorry, but I wasn't sure about what. When I first met Leon I'd made a god of him, then later I'd made a goblin. The truth was that he sat somewhere in the middle of the two, just like all of us.

Are we done? he asked me.

Yeah, I said. I stood up. Will I see you at the club, or do you want me to quit right away?

He frowned, remembering. I wondered if he'd only asked me to stop working there out of spite. I hoped that he had. No, he said. Not right away.

I decided that answer would do, at least for now. I lifted my hand in a pointless wave, but Leon was rolling another cigarette, and didn't look up.

2 1

I had been wrong about Leon. He didn't tell the whole
smoking area about Nim's pregnancy. After that day
at his flat, he did very little talking at all. He stum-
bled around the club with the same absent look on his
face that he'd had when I first told him about the baby,
with that same far-off expression. Any time I spoke to
him, he looked past me, only semi-processing whatever
it was I had to say, if he was processing it at all. Overnight
he became a troubling figure, lurching on the edge of
the dance floor, perpetually alone. Sure, it had long been
commonplace for Leon to take things too far at the club,
to end the night speaking nonsense or else passed out

somewhere other than his bed. But for each night he'd spent off his head he'd made up for with another night in which he was appallingly dynamic, in which he oozed sex appeal, in which his sly jokes could stir a smile in anyone, even Carlos. Even, very occasionally, me.

But after I told him about Nim, there were no more of the latter nights. That side of Leon was swallowed up by ketamine, by the little blue pills that I assumed to be Valium. He hit the downers harder than I'd ever seen. It worried me. For weeks I looked on from behind the bar, I followed him about the dance floor with my eyes. I waited for him to set his sights on a new girl, to get swept up in a crush that would pull him out of his dark hole, even if only for a night, for an hour. For the first time in all the years I'd known Leon, I prayed for him to get laid. But the weeks grew to a month, and no girl came. He wasn't looking at the faces in the crowd, not really. His body was there in the club, but not the rest of him.

Then even his body was there less and less. He stopped showing up every night we were open, and came only every second night, then every third. At first I took that as a good sign. I thought he had finally recognised there was a problem, and was trying to distance himself from the party. What he was actually doing was taking the same amount of drugs, or more, alone in his flat. I found this out one night when I'd called to ask where he was, and he'd garbled some response that I knew meant he was high. I was amazed he'd picked up my call at all. I was stood on the street outside the club with the phone to my ear, having left Nim inside serving. The night was orange, shop fronts and street lights burning up the dark sky. I could make out a few stars towards the seafront, after the light pollution bled to black over the sea. Leon was saying something I couldn't make sense of. There were muffled voices in the background of the call, the din of American accents. I thought that meant he was in company, until I heard the jingle of a theme song and understood it was only his television. I didn't like the idea of him getting on it alone. Leon was a social creature, a performer; he thrived on an audience. He turned towards other people's attention like a sunflower to the light.

Maybe I should have gone over that night, should have checked in on him. Maybe if I had, things would have turned around. Instead, I told him to get his arse down to the club.

I'm gonna kill you, I said, if you don't beat me to it.

I hung up. I couldn't have left Nim alone behind the bar to check on Leon, even if I'd wanted to. She was five months pregnant, and though she never complained about working, I knew from sleeping with her at night that she got cramps in her legs from standing too long. Sometimes she'd wake in the dark, gasping in agony, and I'd stretch her muscles out for her by cycling her legs or pulling on her ankles. I continued to want her to stop working the bar, and she continued to refuse. I'd suggested she could do something else for the club – send emails, keep accounts – but we both knew it wouldn't suit her. She got antsy if she was stuck inside too long. Times she wasn't sleeping, she was swimming or eating or wandering around the city. Nim didn't own a smartphone, and she only watched television when I did. All the same, I tried hard to persuade her. I was worried she was going to exhaust herself.

What kind of pregnant woman works in a nightclub? I asked her.

This one, she said. She was glowering at me. I still exist for myself, Jules. I still need some kind of a life. It's alright for you, coming and going as you want, always with something on your mind, only to be handed a baby in the summer. In the meantime, I'll just sit here and rot.

I thought she was being harsh. I hadn't meant it like that, and she knew. All the same, I apologised. That was the easiest approach with Nim. I couldn't stand up to her. She was too sharp; she had an answer for everything. We were bickering more and more then, and always it was me who backed down first. Another thing we'd argued about was whether to go official with our plans for my raising the baby. In my research, I'd read that if I wanted to legally adopt I should apply now to the courts. I'd called up a number I found online, and spoken to a social worker about it. I'd been sent various forms to fill out, and told I would need to arrange a flat visit and a series of interviews, with both Nim and myself, before I could be approved. The baby would be allowed to live with me from birth, I was assured, in a fostering scenario, but the adoption, and therefore my parental rights, would take much longer to be finalised. I wrote notes while I was on the phone, and afterwards I took them to Nim, so I wouldn't get anything wrong. I hadn't yet told my parents about the baby, and I was keen to be able to lay out the legalities for them, too. I knew they'd be more likely to approve if the whole scenario was thoroughly researched. My parents believed in institutions, they liked everything above board.

Fuck that, Nim said, when I presented her with the notes. I'm not speaking to any social worker.

Why not?

I'm not having them nose around in my past. I'll sign whatever you want. But I'm not speaking to anyone.

I don't think that's possible, Nim. They have to be convinced I'm not bribing you.

Oh, please. I'll just have the baby, pass it to you, and move out. I'll put your name on the birth certificate, instead of a father, so you'll have full parental rights. Simple.

I looked that up later, and understood that Nim had done some of her own research. I'd thought of her as someone uninterested in logistics, in the pointless admin of being alive. But she was right; since 2014, it was law that both partners in a gay couple could be listed on a birth certificate. Still, I was concerned about the early days after the baby was born, before we could get to a registry office. I told her this, and she flashed me her hardest look in response, the one that made me shrink inside myself.

I'm not speaking to any social worker, she repeated. There's no way.

Once or twice I had suspected that Nim was shrouding her past in secrecy on purpose, playing up the mystery as a way to amuse herself. I imagined her then as the wilful middle child, with a trampoline in the garden. Probably she'd run away for attention, her parents left bickering behind the net curtains about what to do, half fretful and half relieved to have her gone. This fantasy was ungenerous, I knew. Besides, I could only buy into it for a moment. Nim had never struck me as a showboat, or a fibber. It seemed more likely, knowing Nim, that her past was bleaker than I ever could have imagined. This did not, however, stop me from *trying* to imagine. I was curious, and in my curiosity I conjured up all kinds of trauma for Nim. I had a little fun with it, found brief spurts of satisfaction. I would convince myself of some grim aspect of Nim's past, then feel proud to have cracked it, to have deepened my limited understanding of her. It was no more than delusion, but delusion was better than nothing.

Nim's twenty-week scan was some days after our conversation about the social worker. I'd been to all her midwife appointments, waited outside on the fold-up chairs while she went in to have her bloods done, to give a urine sample. For the scan, I begged Nim to let me into the room with her.

I don't know, she said. I barely even looked last time.

That's fine, I said. You don't have to look, but I'd like to.

She'd shrugged, and I knew that was as close as I would get to an agreement.

It was dark in the hospital room, and it smelled like mouthwash. The sonographer kept calling Nim by her real name, which is Mina. I'd learned that at the midwife appointments, when they called it through the waiting room. In the scan, Nim shot me a look.

She prefers Nim, I said quickly.

The sonographer consulted her notes. She was a little abrupt, I thought. Then again, it was late in the day. You must be the wife, she said. Jules, is it?

Nim spoke up quickly. We're not married, actually. It should say partner.

The sonographer checked her notes again, flicked an eyebrow. She picked up a tube of jelly and gave it a single shake, to force the contents to one end. Nim, taking the hint, pulled her shirt up. The sonographer squeezed some jelly onto the bare skin. I noticed goosebumps prick up across Nim's stomach. The sonographer pressed a probe into Nim's bump, and the sound was like driving down a motorway, the window slightly open. I looked at Nim in the electric light of the screen, but she wouldn't make eye contact. Her gaze stayed cast down the whole time. That was why she'd never invited me into one of her midwife appointments, I thought. It was because she was worried I'd give us away. I'd been a part of the baby's future this whole time, and Nim had made sure of it.

I turned my attention to the screen. There he was, clear as a satellite. The sonographer pointed everything out with the cursor of her mouse: the limbs, the spine, the major organs. She kept glancing at Nim, wondering why it was she wouldn't look up. In an effort to distract the sonographer, I asked lots of questions, humming my acknowledgement of her answers. I stared at the baby. I breathed the word Wow, over and over. Wow, wow. I was trying to make Nim and I come across as normal, as happy. I could see that was what the sonographer expected us to be. I even reached out to Nim and took her hand. It was limp, a little clammy. She didn't hold mine back, but I hardly cared. I was absorbed in pleasing the sonographer, in trying to comprehend the baby on the screen. Wow, I kept saying.

When it was done, the lights came up and the sonographer left the room to print a photo for us. Nim pulled a few sheets from the blue roll by the hospital bed and wiped the jelly from her stomach. It was only then that I noticed her eyes looked stung. I let her shuffle off the bed, trying to work out what to say. Then the sonographer came back, silvery printouts tucked into a plastic wallet, and I was again distracted, forcing enough jubilance to make up for the both of us. I still have those prints somewhere around here.

2 2

I take the baby into town. It's our first time leaving the flat together. I tell myself we're going for a walk, when of course we're going to look for Nim. I drop by the club, which has been locked up for weeks now, a chain snaking through the stack of metal barriers propped against the main doors so that nobody can steal them. I weave through the streets, the scrubby green spaces, everywhere packed with tourists now that it's summer: great hordes of people with nowhere to be, lingering, deciding whether or not to get a pint, to get an ice cream. There's no sign of her. I look in the windows of shops. I sweep my eyes up the opposite side of the road, then back down the side I'm walking on. I have the pebble she gave me in my pocket, and as I look for her I run my thumb over its smooth, cool surface.

I check on the baby, nestled in his sling against my front. It's hot and I'm sweating on him, but he doesn't care, he sleeps. I take him to the beach. I want him to breathe the sea air, get away from the petrol fumes around the shopping centre. The seafront is busier than town. I wouldn't be able to spot her here even if she wanted to be found, even if we were on the phone and she was waving to me, her towel laid out on the pebbles. Why would she be here, anyway? I know her well enough to know that she would not be sunbathing with a crowd of revellers, after everything: dub blasting out a portable speaker, a plastic cup of Pimm's warming by her elbow.

I've filled her voicemail, but still I keep calling. I'm unsure how I'll be able to go on, not knowing if she's safe. I'm unsure how I'll raise her baby, not knowing. What will I tell him? You had a mother, but I drove her away. I was blind, and the only way she could make me see was by disappearing. I'd like to be angry with Nim – maybe that would be easier – but I'm too angry with myself.

On the seafront, crossing the promenade is like crossing a road. I have to wait for the stream of tourists to die down in order to cut between them. Families are queue-ing for the carousel, children with massive dummies made of sugar. I watch a seagull steal an entire hot dog out the hand of a little boy. The birds get bigger every year, and more brash with it. The boy bursts into tears. The parents try to console him, try not to laugh. They look contented. I watch the seagull tip its head back and attempt to force the hot dog down its gullet in one. The bun has been discarded, lying open by the seagull's putty-coloured feet. I'm holding a muslin over the sling in an attempt to create shade. I keep thinking I should go home, before the baby starts to stir, but I am yet to turn around. An image arrives in my mind of a seagull pluck-ing him right out the sling, flying off. I remember that day on the pier with Nim, watching the starlings. My brain isn't working normally. I can't hold on to one thought; everything rushes in together. Other times, it switches off completely.

The parents of the child with the stolen hot dog have noticed the baby, how small he is. Little freshy, they're saying. Well done on getting out.

I nod in thanks, but I don't want to chat. I keep walk-ing to get past them. I'm on the pebbles now, I've started picking my way down to the sea. A midwife came to weigh the baby this morning, and he's dropped from his birth weight. She assured me this is normal, but still I thought I was going to vomit. She went through the questionnaire that she usually asks mothers on their three-day check, but most of the questions didn't apply. She asked me about my mood, and I told her I was alright, considering. The midwife knows about my situation, but we didn't speak of Nim, outside of that word. Considering. I didn't tell the midwife that when I'm holding the baby, I can sense his reluctance. I didn't tell her that every time he looks at me, I know he's looking for his mother.

At the shore I kick my shoes off and walk into the water. It seems like something Nim would do. If I can't find her, perhaps I'll just have to become her. It's a bad idea, really. The getting in, I mean. I'm unsteady on the slippery pebbles, and I know that if I fall with the baby in the sling it could be disastrous. The bottom few inches of my skirt gets soaked. The water isn't even nice; it's soupy, with a scum of dirt floating on top. I get out and kick my shoes back on, not bothering with the socks. The baby, miraculously, is still asleep. I peer in at him for a while, check his breathing. I slip two fingers behind his neck to make sure he isn't too hot. We walk home, finally. I'm uncomfortable, wet feet shoved into trainers folded down at the heels, drips running down my legs like I've wet myself. When we get into the lift, I notice in the silence that the baby has her snore.

23

May was the hottest on record. Nim and I spent a lot of time on the beach. We'd catch the bus out to Saltdean, to Seaford, and pitch up for the whole day. Nim relaxed when we were outside. I always felt like my flat was too small for her. Not that she needed a mansion, more that she couldn't be contained by any walls at all. When we were inside she jittered her legs, she got bored easily, she could be surly with me. She was too big for my mundane existence – I'd understood that from the beginning – but the more pregnant she got, the more true it became. Sometimes I let myself consider a future, after the baby was born, with her in it. I imagined her taking on the role of fun aunt, or part-time dad. I could picture Nim and the child breaking into the bumper cars on the pier, or going down to the Level to learn how to skate. She'd bring them home late on a school night, buzzing from sugar, with scraped-up knees. I'd answer the door with a face on, pretending to be cross, though I wouldn't be able to keep it up for long.

Not that Nim and I ever talked about what would happen after. We talked about her labour a lot, how she wanted to give birth in a pool, without music. How she was afraid of forceps, and anything else they might stick inside her to help the baby out. But that was all. It was as if the birth was the last thing that would happen to either of us. Chronologically, we spoke of nothing further along. I didn't know if she would want to hold the baby after they were born, or if she would want to see them regularly as they grew. It wasn't a simple conversation to bring up with Nim, how much she intended to see her child. I suspected she didn't really know, and was waiting to find out. She expected the answer to become clear of its own accord, and I had no choice but to expect that too. Perhaps it was true, also, that I didn't ask because I didn't want to know. I was afraid of the child loving Nim more than me, even then. I was afraid that, if she stayed in the picture, the baby would never feel like mine. But the idea of a clean separation, of no contact between us, was painful as well.

She told me once that she expected an invite to all the birthday parties, but she was laughing when she spoke, like she didn't fully mean it.

Whenever I remembered Nim's red eyes in her scan appointment, I got nervous. We still hadn't discussed how anguished she'd looked that day. We'd walked home in silence, where she'd taken a nap and got up acting like nothing had happened. I knew I was a coward for not asking why she was upset, but if I pushed her to tell me that she was having second thoughts about giving up the baby, I would have to respond, and it would all be over. I was always trying not to put Nim on the spot, or make her talk about her feelings. I told myself it was because I couldn't risk annoying her, but really I think I was afraid of her telling me something that I didn't want to hear. Nim was a puzzle to me, and as unnerving as that was, I was never quite sure if I wanted her solved.

It was on the beach when Nim finally confided in me about her past. I think it had to do with the fact we'd been together all day, my attention fully on her. At the flat I was always working on my laptop, or running out the door to the club, or cooking her something. The beach placated me. I wasn't good in the heat; all I could do was lie there. It started with Nim bringing up Leon, which was not usual for her. Always it had been me, in Buddie's, who'd made him the centre of conversation.

On the beach, Nim asked if I thought he might clean up eventually, become a good dad.

I doubt it, I said, my eyes closed to the sun. He seems pretty certain he doesn't want to be involved.

D'you think his mother knows?

Rita? No. If she did, she'd have called me to say how callous I am for doing this to him. As if he's played no part in it himself.

D'you think he's told anyone at all?

I wiped some sweat from my brow. No, I said. Usually he would have. He'd have gone all poor-me, and told the whole world. But he's in a bad state these days. I don't think he's socialising much.

Doesn't he have any close friends?

He's never prioritised friendship, as far as I can see.

He seems lonely to me.

I shielded my eyes with a hand, and squinted at her. The horizon was vibrating in the heat. Lonely? I said. There was a new girl in his bed every night, until about a month ago.

Exactly. Nobody sticks around.

I scoffed. Can you blame them? I asked.

That night we slept together, said Nim, he wouldn't leave. I kept dropping hints, but he begged me to let him stay. We were in my narrow single, and I knew neither of us would get any sleep. I was pissed off with him, too, because of the condom, and because I regretted the whole thing. But he wouldn't have it. He clung to me all night, trying not to fall out the bed, rather than just getting up and going home. In the morning he still wanted to stick around. I was rude. I told him I had somewhere to be, though it was obvious I didn't. I got the money off him for the morning-after pill and then I kicked him out. He looked so sad when he left, and I had the feeling it happened like that a lot, with the other girls. He'd manage to get into bed with someone when they were drunk, then in the morning they'd be disgusted with him.

And whose fault is that?

I'm not saying it's not his fault, Jules. But it's sad. He's desperate for some real connection. It's the curse of the straight man, don't you think? He wants a woman to offload all his problems onto, but he can't offer the same level of emotional support in return, so the relationship never starts, or else it ends badly, like with you and him. That's the cycle. Agreed, he's slimy, he should be going for women his own age. I'm not condoning that. But he works in a student club, and he's lazy.

I laughed. It came from me like a bark. He works in a student club so he can fuck students, Nim.

I thought it was a student club before he took it over?

I had to admit that was true. Still, it seemed beside the point. I think you're being kind, I said.

Is that so bad?

I peered at her. What are you trying to say?

Nim shrugged. She was sat cross-legged in her cotton underwear, leaning back into her arms, her palms spread out on the pebbles. Sometimes I think you flatten people, she said. She spoke quietly, but I heard.

What d'you mean? I asked.

It's supposed to be Leon's club, said Nim, but he's got no responsibilities at all. OK, maybe he'd fuck them up, but you don't even give him the opportunity. It's infantilising. Now he's having a kid, and you're taking full care of it. He didn't even know I was pregnant until all that was decided. We totally bypassed the idea that he could ever be a proper dad.

Yeah, because he couldn't.

I'm not disagreeing with you, I'm just saying. It must suck for him. Even if he's never wanted kids, it's the whole presumption of it.

I rolled my lips together. Nim, I said. Do I flatten you?

She was looking at the water, as if deciding whether or not to go in. I know you think I'm just some damaged kid, she said.

I don't think that, I protested.

We're not equals, in your head. You and me.

Of course we are.

She turned to look at me, eyes sharp enough to cut. You know I had a crush on you, she said, when I first met you?

Occasionally I got the sense that Nim said things out of boredom, for a reaction. This was one of those times. No you didn't, I said.

Exactly. You'd never even consider it. You think of yourself as a mother figure, as someone who's looking after me.

I *am* looking after you, Nim.

Maybe I'm looking after you, too, she said.

I pulled my neck in.

See? said Nim. You hate the idea of it.

I could say the same to you, I said. You're always resisting my help.

That's because your help *feels* like charity. You think of me as weak, and in everything you do for me, that comes across. Nothing is mutual with you. Why do you think I'm weak, though? Is it because I'm young, or because I'm poor, or because I'm pregnant?

Nim.

What? Tell me.

I swallowed. I have no idea where you came from, I said. You've never told me anything about your background.

It shouldn't matter.

Shouldn't it? I worry about you.

You worry about me, you worry about Leon. You don't think anyone can stand on their own two feet, except yourself. Imagine if I dared to worry about you, Jules. You'd be so offended you'd never speak to me again.

Nim stood up. She was fast for someone so pregnant. Where are you going? I asked. We're halfway through a conversation.

I'm getting in, she said. I need to cool off. You coming?

No, I said. I'll be here.

24

Nim swam for fifteen minutes, maybe more. I sifted pebbles through my hands and thought about how she was right: I was determined to think of myself as above other people. Was this why I wanted a baby? Was this why other people kept on having babies? Despite the strain of pregnancy, the agony of birth, despite the terror of unknowable love, we wanted so badly to see ourselves in somebody else, and we wanted to have control over that person. We wanted a chance to build a destiny, from day one. We wanted a new start.

I'd brought a bottle of water, and I gulped some down. It was warm, and tasted like plastic.

Pass it here, said Nim.

I hadn't even noticed she was out. She stood over me while she drank, the corner of her elbow blocking out the sun, the light coming through the plastic making feathery waves on my legs, on the towels. Her belly was round as a buoy. From underneath, looking up, I noticed thin stretch marks drawing upwards, the skin pulled thin enough that it had taken on a lustre. Her white knickers were soaked translucent, her pubic hair a big dark scribble. She was seven months pregnant, and her swimming costume no longer fit.

How was it? I asked her.

Nice, she said. I think the baby noticed the temperature change.

Nim sat down next to me. Her legs were bent loosely, in one direction, underneath her. She seemed softer now, and I hoped the sea had acquitted me. Here, she said. Feel.

Her belly was slippery and cool, the flesh surprisingly firm. I rested my hands on the table of her, and she picked them up and moved them lower, slightly left. I couldn't feel anything. I closed my eyes and waited. The kick was not the single, poking movement I'd imagined, but a sliding, continuous hardness that came once and then again, muscular as an eel beneath the skin. The first time it happened, I jerked my hands away in surprise, only to place them back immediately, so as not to miss anything more. I sat with my hands on Nim for ages, long after the baby had stopped moving.

My mother's pregnancy with me was cryptic, said Nim.

What's that? I asked.

It's when you don't know you're pregnant.

All the way through?

Nim nodded. It's rare, but it happens. They say it might be psychological. You're in such strong denial that your body doesn't show any symptoms.

And then what, you just suddenly start giving birth?

Pretty much, said Nim. My mum went to A&E with stomach cramps, and they told her she was in labour. Nobody believed her, after. My dad was married to someone else, with young kids of his own, and when my mother told him about me he decided she'd known all along, that the whole thing was some big ploy to ruin his life. The irony is that it didn't ruin his life at all; it barely touched it. But it ruined hers.

Nim, I said. Don't say that.

It's true. My mother didn't want to be a mother, especially not like that.

Well, what did she want?

Nim clicked her tongue, looked out at the horizon. Men, she said.

Men?

Love, marriage, validation. I fucked up the first great romance of her life, and she always resented me for that.

What's she like? I asked. Nim had given me an opening, and suddenly it seemed reasonable to probe. I had
the sense that she needed to talk about her mother, she'd
needed to for a long time, and now she wouldn't finish
talking until the story was done.

What's she like? echoed Nim, thinking. She loves chat
rooms, and the pub. She's bitter, and very angry. She can
spiral into a huge rage over the smallest thing. She once
used the remote as a baton to wreck the TV, and she got
cuts all up her wrists, from the glass. It's lucky she's
so tiny, or she could do some real damage. She's weak
though, she hardly eats a thing. She had this rule for a
while, when I was a kid, that she'd only eat if a man
cooked for her or took her out. She could go days without a meal.

My god, I said.

She has this scar down the left side of her face, said
Nim. And one of her eyes is lazy. She was in a car crash
when I was eight or nine. She'd left me home alone to go
on a date. This guy she was seeing was drunk, but she got
in the car with him anyway. He lived out of town, on the
badly lit country roads, and that was where it happened.
I woke to an empty flat, and took myself to school. That
wasn't unusual, but still I knew something was wrong.
At that age, I thought I was psychic. I thought I could
predict, by this heavy feeling in my knuckles, when
something bad was going to happen. I had that feeling all

day, and when I got home she was covered in bandages, totally out of it on meds, having left the hospital without being discharged. The guy never even called her back. I was so young, I thought she might learn. I was always waiting for her to give it up.

Did you ever ask her to?

When I was little, I'd beg her to stay home but she'd say she was going out to get me a new dad. She'd make like she was doing it for me. I always remember how she smelled when she said that: of chewing gum and body spray and the shot of vodka she did before she left, to loosen herself for the men. I wasn't bothered about having a father, and I told her over and over. My biggest secret was that I liked girls. I knew that by six or seven, and it was the thing always playing on my mind. A father, I could take or leave. Besides, I had no hope for the men my mother chose.

I realised then how naïve I'd been, to make a game of imagining Nim's childhood. How naïve I'd been to expect, at the beginning of this conversation, that she'd be able to express her past to me fully, that she'd be able to talk and talk until the story was done. There was too much of it for that. She'd lived a whole life before me, and some part of her remained there still, inexpressible.

When I was fifteen, said Nim, my mother met Phil. He moved in with us right away. He'd sit around watching the shopping channel while my mother worked, allowing his gross friends to come and go. Once I woke in the middle of the night and there was a man in my bedroom, some mate of Phil's, just watching me while I slept. I screamed, and he backed out slowly. I don't like to think what would've happened if I hadn't woken up. Phil knew about it, too. I could tell the next morning, when I confronted him. I reckon he'd encouraged it, maybe some money had even changed hands.

I felt sick. Did you tell your mother? I asked.

Nim shrugged. I can't remember. There were lots of things like that, far too many to keep track of. She put up with all of it. He was much worse to her than to me. Much, much worse.

I couldn't look at Nim then. My hands were wet from the heat.

Phil was an ex-policeman, said Nim. He'd lost his job for misconduct. That was why he had nowhere to live, no money coming in. I don't know the details of why he was fired, but I could make a fair guess. He put my mother in hospital multiple times. I always told the staff the real reason she was there. They believed me, but they said there was nothing they could do unless my mother admitted to it. She wouldn't, of course. She called me a liar so many times, in front of so many people, that eventually I just gave up. I figured if she wanted to die, I had to let her. I moved out, basically.

Where did you go?

Remember Beth, whose mum had IVF?

I nodded.

I stayed with her most nights, said Nim, trying to avoid being home. I was in love with Beth, is the truth. Some days I think I still am. She'd pull her mattress onto the floor, next to the camp bed I slept in, so we could spend all night straddling and kissing each other. I was always the boyfriend, Beth the girlfriend. She'd give me tips on how to use my tongue, and I'd follow her advice religiously. She lived mostly off sweets, and she refused to brush her teeth before bed, so her mouth always tasted of Starburst. She lost a tooth in front of me once, and there was a big grey hole in it.

I smiled at the detail. Nim was smiling too, just a little, remembering.

Beth was like my mum, said Nim. In that she always had a different boyfriend. But still we'd do our kissing. I thought she was just going through the motions, that one day she'd stop dating boys and admit that we could be together properly. Then when we were seventeen she got a boyfriend in the year above, and the day he moved away for university Beth dropped out of school and went with him. I was pissed when she told me she was leaving. I lost my grip, just like my mother used to, and kicked the Perspex wall of a bus stop until I sprained my ankle. Beth was always top of the class, I'd looked up to her for years, and now she was abandoning school for some guy. Not only that: she was abandoning me. No woman would ever love me as much as they loved their man. I learned that at seventeen, the day Beth left. It wasn't long after that I left too, hobbled on my bad ankle down to the station. I didn't tell my mother I was leaving, and we've had no contact since.

You mean you ran away?

Nim looked at me closely, for a long time. She studied my face, brows knit, as if doubting that I had listened to a single word she'd said. She tutted. No, Jules, she said. I didn't run. I left. I walked out. There's a difference, see?

25

We went home soon after Nim told me about her mother. We jangled around the flat, not knowing how to interact. I think we were avoiding each other. When one of us walked into a room, the other would soon leave it. I spent a long time making a salad, dicing all the vegetables I could find in the fridge, shaking a dressing together in a jam jar, adding a tin of chickpeas for protein. I kept finding myself picturing Nim asleep, a man's shadow stretched long over her bed. I wanted to rush through to the living room and hold her, but I knew she despised anything like pity. Instead, I made her salad. When it was ready, it tasted of nothing. I served

Nim a huge portion all the same, but when I brought it into the living room, where we always ate, she wasn't in there. I could hear a noise like an electric toothbrush, and I followed it into the bathroom, where I found her going over her shaved head with a set of clippers. Our eyes met in the mirror. She'd done the top and the sides of her hair already, so the towel she was standing on was scattered with clumps of dark fuzz. In the late sun coming in through the window, tiny strands of hair rocked as they fell, flickering gold in the light.

I made a gross dinner, I said.

She smiled, without looking happy. Great, she said. I'll be through.

You want me to do the back?

Yeah, actually. If that's OK.

She passed the clippers to me. Stood behind her, I drew a clean stripe up her head, like a skunk. I had to stand on my tiptoes. Her skin smelled of sweat and salt. Or maybe that was her hair, coming away. I thought of Nim on the beach earlier, accusing me of glorifying myself as her mother figure. Yet it was impossible, sliding the clippers over Nim's head, not to conclude that she had somehow sought me out as her mother's replacement.

As if Nim could see inside my mind, she asked me a question which convinced me that she too was comparing me, in that moment, to her mother. You don't want romantic love, she said. Do you, Jules?

I kept shaving as I considered it. I'd never asked myself this question in such simple terms. I intended to answer truthfully, but still when I spoke I wondered if I was lying, if I was telling her what she wanted to hear. She'd read me as the opposite of her mother, I understood, and had come to rely on that as fact. No, I said. I don't think I do.

I'd thought this answer would please Nim, but her expression flashed strange. Some emotion passed over her face which I couldn't decipher, so fast that as soon as I noticed it, it was gone. She settled her mouth, then nodded. Romance is given such importance, she said. It scares me, the amount that people become willing to lose. When I met you, you seemed totally self-sufficient. I was fascinated.

I ran a hand over Nim's hair, so see if I could pick up on any unevenness. She wasn't looking in the mirror anymore, but elsewhere. Her head was satisfying to touch, like the neck of a horse. I was pleased by what she'd said. It had never occurred to me that the way I wanted to appear to people was the way that I actually appeared.

That's why I chose you for the baby, I think.

You want the baby to be my greatest love, I said.

Sure, said Nim. But I don't want you to lose yourself, either. It's no example.

That's the hard part, I said. My parents lost themselves when they had me. Or, they lost the people they could have been.

I went back in on Nim's hair, started smoothing it over with long and possibly unnecessary strokes. When she spoke her voice was louder than before, with no shake in it. That's why I avoid talking with you about what will happen after the birth, she said. I know it'll involve you giving me something, money for rent or whatever, which in turn will make me feel like I've left something behind, like I've lost something. Not the baby, necessarily, but some essential part of myself.

Nim, I said. You won't be the same person you were before, after this. You know that, don't you? You're paying a price for the baby. Your body is paying that price, and your mind too. I should get the chance to pay you back, or at least try, don't you agree?

Nim sniffed. You're thinking about it wrong, she said. Why does everything have to be transactional?

Because of the world we live in, I said.

But that's what's made everyone so lonely in the first place, Jules. We give up our time in exchange for money, so we don't have the energy for friendship, don't have space for anyone who isn't directly useful to us. We partner off, we combine incomes, we make babies, we buy a house. We look out for one person only, and they look out for us, until the pressure gets too much, and it all falls apart. It's not working, not for anyone, as far as I can see.

Are we that person, to each other?

I don't know why I asked that. The words just flew out. Nim seemed to get nervous at the suggestion. She gave a small shrug. I'd turned the clippers off, and the silence swelled. Maybe right now, she said. But not for much longer.

26

I woke early the following morning, to my ringtone. When the voice on the phone told me they were calling from the Accident & Emergency department at the hospital, my first thought was that Leon was dead. Leon was not dead, but he'd come close. He'd been found by a neighbour who'd noticed that his front door was slightly ajar. The neighbour had stepped into the flat to see if Leon was in, only to discover him collapsed in the hallway, lying in a puddle of fluorescent orange liquid. The neighbour had initially taken the liquid for piss, though it was in fact spilled Fanta.

Leon, at the tail end of a three-day bender, so wrecked he'd hardly been able to walk, had gone to the corner shop for a drink. Later, when I asked him, he had no recollection of going to the shop, nor of the entire day that led up to his collapse. A teenager who worked behind the counter at Leon's local had told the paramedics that, yes, Leon had been in to buy a Fanta, and was walking in an odd, off-balance way. He'd tried to buy a small bottle of vodka, too, though he'd brought no money with him. The teenager, taking pity on Leon, had allowed him to take the Fanta for free. According to the doctors, the sugar in the Fanta ingested by Leon may actually have stopped his heart from entirely giving out. There was nothing in his system otherwise but cocaine, Valium and alcohol. Leon had suffered a heart attack just as he stepped inside, falling in his flat and leaving the door open behind him. This last was another detail that had potentially saved his life. Anyone else, I told Nim later, would surely have died. Leon was able to push everything to its absolute limit, and still manage to drag himself out the other side.

I went to visit him in hospital, the same day I was called. It was strange going there without Nim, bypassing the maternity ward for cardiac, to find my ex-husband hooked up to a drip, slowly coming around from his overdose. I hoped none of the staff recognised me. Leon was in his own room, asleep under a papery sheet, his lips so chapped they looked scrubbed with chalk. There were a few leaflets on his bedside, about drug abuse and rehab. I flicked through them while Leon slept. His room was on a high-up floor, with a big window. The day was overcast, one of those tropical summer days when it needs to rain. In the dull light, the city sprawled bigger and greyer than it ever felt on the ground. Cars packed the roads like aphids. The glass on the tower blocks reflected back the grey streets lined with little grey houses, the railway lines. Any green patches appeared dense and bushy, dark as rainforest. The sea was green too, a long strip of swamp. I scoured the view for people, and found some, each figure floating along the pavement like a spore. How small we seemed from up there, how lonely, how inconsequential. Say Leon's heart had stopped for good that morning, I thought. What would that have meant, in the scheme of everything? Say he'd worn a condom when he slept with Nim. What then? One less solitary mite, down there on the pavements, or else one more. That was all, really.

Oh please, Jules. What are you reading those for?

I looked up, and there was Rita. I was still holding the leaflets. You don't think rehab's a good idea? I asked.

Rita waved a hand through the air. It's a phase, she said. We all went through one.

He's pushing forty, Rita. I don't think that word applies.

I know how old my son is, darling.

I clicked my tongue. Your son needs help, I said. Look at him.

Rita didn't look at Leon, but at the floor. It was true that he was a chilling sight: the blue lace of his eyelids, the dead lips, the tubes pumping pale pink fluid into his veins. I glanced back at Rita, and I saw that her face had slightly crumpled. She gave a mewing sound, very small, like she'd been winded. Rita, I said. I gave her a hug. It was the first time I'd touched her in years. She broke down the moment I put my arms around her, heaving breaths into my ear. Her body writhed, and I had to grip her tight to keep us standing.

I can't do this, she wailed. I can't do it, Jules.

I just held her, waiting for her to calm. The change had come suddenly, and had taken me by surprise. When she'd walked into the room she'd looked as put together as always, a thin line of blue metallic applied to her eyelids. Initially, I'd read her as undeterred by Leon's state. Rita had partied in the New York fashion scene all through her twenties, and it made sense to me that she'd seen this kind of thing before. It wasn't until I'd noticed that she was unable to look at her son that I knew.

He's all I've got, she said into my ear. He's all I've ever had. He's my everything, see, so I gave him everything. I can't lose him now. I'll have nothing left.

I held Rita, and as I did so it occurred to me that you needed more than two people in a family. The jump from two to one was too small; it could happen in an instant. She was crying still, and I hushed her, shuffling from foot to foot as we hugged, so that together we rocked gently.

Leon's voice was raspy, and the word came like a cough. Cute, he said.

Rita and I jumped apart. I don't know how long Leon had been awake, watching us from his bed. He was smirking. How he still managed to irritate me in his condition was impressive. I shook my head. You alright? I said.

Been better, said Leon.

I can see that.

Leon looked at his mother, who was trying to pull herself together now, dabbing the leaked mascara from her upper cheeks with the pad of her little finger. She took in a frayed breath. Leon gave her his charming look, big-eyed. He was her baby, and he knew. I'd judged Rita for years for spoiling her son, for dismissing his every fuck up as the innocent behaviour of a much younger person, for enabling him. But it was true that I did not have a child of my own, that I did not know forgiveness when it came to an adult you had raised, when blaming them for anything ultimately meant blaming yourself. Besides, the whole world was kind to men. The whole world spoiled them. Rita was only one person, responsible for her single part.

She went to him now, took his cheeks in one hand and squeezed the skin together so his mouth puckered. There was even less to him than usual, almost no flesh at all. She kissed him on the forehead, then she let go of his face and gave him a tiny slap on the cheek. She pointed at him, her head ducked to his level, so she could look him right in the eye. You've just aged me ten years, she said. You're lucky I love you, Leon. I wouldn't take that from anyone else.

I was stood at the far end of the room, just watching. I didn't know why I was there, on the outskirts of this small family. I folded my arms. We were really worried, I said.

I can see that, said Leon. When was the last time you two hugged?

I cocked an eyebrow. It was unrelenting, the way we were with each other. He winked. You seem happy to be alive, I said.

He was still giving his stupid smirk, but I caught a flash in his eye then, I was sure: something like recognition. Let's keep it that way, I said. No more of this, Leon.

Without looking at Rita, I placed the leaflets in his lap. Have a read of these, I said. When you're up to it.

I stayed in the hospital for another hour after that. I'd brought yoghurts with chocolate sprinkles, crisps that looked like onion rings, and a cheap packet of cupcakes iced with pastel-coloured dots of glaze. In food, Leon had the tastes of a child. Still, he didn't touch the snacks. He said he had no appetite. He drank water from a plastic cup that I fetched from the filter in reception, but took in nothing else. He was drowsy, and over time his shameless attitude began to flag. The smirk eventually slipped from his face, along with any remote hint of colour, and he started responding to everything with either a shrug or a one-word answer. A doctor came to do some checks, and by then Leon's eyes were closing of their own accord. I tapped the leaflets one more time, to remind him, before I left. Rita was picking the icing from a cupcake, staring off out the window.

2 7

I took the long way home from the hospital, walked
through the balmy streets with my headphones on,
the noise of the city entirely drowned out. I thought
of the home videos I'd seen of Leon as a child, and of
the hole in his heart which I'd considered for years as
an ironic detail in the story of our marriage. In the
green behind my building, I found my vision getting
blurry. I took my headphones off, and paused by the
stone fountain to cry. There were two teenage girls in
school uniform sitting on the fountain ledge, taking
selfies with their hands held up in front of their faces.
They'd just had their nails done. One girl had gone for

pink tiger stripes, and the other had a tiny hole punched through the top corner of the thumbnail, a silver hoop threaded through, with a tiny blue die dangling. I offered to take a photo of the girls. They looked at each other in a concerned way, because of my crying, but they accepted. I supposed the urge for documentation was strong enough. I watched the girls in the phone screen, their hands fanned out, their eyes rolled jokily upwards, and I thought: none of us are getting out of here alive, and that's the point.

How was Leon? Nim asked me, when I got into the flat.

Pretty rough. Thinking about rehab, I hope.

I joined her on the far end of the sofa. I wasn't sure if she really wanted to talk about Leon, but I did. I picked up her feet and punched them with a weak fist to get the blood going, as I knew she liked me to do. I told Nim about Leon's IV, about Rita's breakdown, about regretting how I was with Leon when he woke up. I'd been pithy, I knew, a little cold.

I'm always like that with him, I said. It's automatic, and he asks for it. But he just nearly died, Nim. If there was one time to be nice, it was today. I shouldn't have argued with Rita about his going to rehab, either, as if it had nothing to do with him. What if he was awake the whole time, feigning sleep, listening to us?

I'm sure he wasn't, Jules.

You were right, you know, about how I infantilise him. I'm as bad as his mother is. Of course he's been irresponsible with his life, when nobody's ever made him responsible for anything. On my way home just now, I kept asking myself why I let it get to this point. Why didn't I suggest rehab weeks ago, as soon as I noticed him spiralling?

This isn't your fault, Jules.

Not completely, I said. But I think a part of me has relied on his self-sabotage, all these years. I think it makes me feel in control, by comparison. It's been true from the day I met him. I've always craved independence, always loved feeling in charge. My parents never granted me that, but Leon did. I'm not self-sufficient at all, Nim, like you thought I was when we first met. Really, I'm the opposite. I need Leon, so that I can pretend.

I looked at Nim, and I could see by her expression that I'd let her down. I was not the woman she'd anticipated me to be. Just like her mother, I'd relied on a man in order to feel whole. Nim gave a tiny smile, with one half of her mouth. I like that, she said.

I peered at her. It was not what I'd expected her to say.

You like to think that people need you, she said. But you need other people, too. It works both ways, Jules. The same goes for the baby. You know that, right? You'll be more needed in the beginning, but gradually less and less. There may well come a point when you find that you need them more than they need you.

I thought of Rita in the hospital, unable to look. It was not possible, I realised then, to build a new destiny through your child. If you had any control over them at all, which seemed doubtful to me now, it was only in the very early days. After that, you had no choice but to do what you could with the person you were given, and with the person you were yourself. Simply, you had to allow life to happen.

Nim didn't speak for a while. She gnawed at the skin around her fingernails, looking out of the window. D'you think I should get in touch with my mother, Jules?

I studied her, trying to gauge what she wanted me to say. I took in her furred head with the big mouth, the clear eyes, her belly button poking through the cotton of her T-shirt.

You really want my answer?

I asked for it, didn't I?

I don't know about should or shouldn't, I said. But I hope you can. I hope you do.

Nim looked at me for a time. I realised I'd been afraid of her reaction, that a part of me was always a little afraid of her. She was too plain with her truth. Now she smiled at me, abruptly. In her eyes, a glint of mischief. I don't know if you've noticed, she said, but I'm kind of busy right now.

Not now, then. Later. When things are slow.

She laughed. I don't really do slow, she said.

I lifted a shoulder. I could see that she was done talking about her mother, was using humour to deflect, and I was not about to push her any further. Maybe we should try it for a bit, I said. Slowing down. We're getting closer to the end, Nim.

The beginning, you mean.

Her smile had faded, gently.

2 8

Nim did attempt to slow down after our conversation. I, however, failed to heed my own advice. The following weeks were hot and frantic. I'd had no idea that the baby would come early, of course, but still I felt a perpetual and extravagant sense of rush, convinced that time was slipping away from me. I hardly slept, but sat awake half the night, scrolling online stores and marketplaces. I found shopping for the baby difficult; I was too hooked on getting it right. I watched YouTube videos about the best cots, the best high chairs, only to find after my extensive research that I couldn't afford any of it. All the high street clothes were monochrome, shades of greige, and looking at them made my eyes itchy. I wanted a bin bag of secondhand sleepsuits to show up at my front door, faded from the wash and covered in curious stains. That was what love looked like, surely. That was what happened in great, rambling families, where people cared for each other communally. I couldn't offer the baby that. I had no siblings, no cousins, no friends with kids. I couldn't even get pregnant naturally, and there were times I would convince myself this meant I wasn't supposed to have a child after all, that I had cheated and would soon be caught out. At that thought I would get frustrated, finally slam my laptop closed and go to bed in tears.

Another thing I did on my laptop late at night was research rehab centres for Leon. The day before he was due to leave hospital, when he would be driven by Rita to the place I'd found, I let myself into his flat so that I could pack him a suitcase. While I was there, I couldn't help but tidy his squalor. This ended up swallowing three full days. I sweated and scrubbed, drank straight from the tap like an athlete. There was a time when I would have been furious with myself for doting on Leon like this – for again casting myself as the woman in his life who kept up with his chores – but on this occasion I found cleaning his flat cathartic. It was as if I was scrubbing away all the lingering grime of our marriage, all the resentment and missteps, so that when

Leon returned from rehab there would be no trace of me waiting to see him fail. I had the unshakeable feeling, when I left Leon's for the final time, that I would not be back there to visit, not ever.

I went to see my parents and told them, finally, about the baby. I hadn't showered, and my hair was stuck to my face. I kept from my parents how soon Nim was due, because I was ashamed at how long I'd held back the information. When they didn't ask – they were distracted by questions of custody, of paperwork – I felt relieved and then very stupid. The reality was that the longer I took to tell them, the closer the birth would be. As a teenager, I'd always wanted to have something to conceal from my parents, to have somewhere to sneak off to. I remember sitting in my father's office, at thirteen or so, while he was in another room, taking slow turns on his swivel chair and flicking quietly through the nudie calendar he kept tacked to the wall, snacking on Hobnobs I'd stolen from the tin by the kettle. It had felt good then to frolic, to break some small rules. But now I was a grown woman, and sneaking around felt juvenile. I wasn't interested in leading a life that my parents wholly endorsed, but I would've hoped to value my choices enough to be transparent about them.

When I got back to the flat from my parents' house, Nim was in a bad mood, lying on the sofa and drumming her fingers incessantly on the coffee table. I asked her if she needed anything, and she only grunted. Her moods were increasingly unpredictable. I blamed her unsteady hormones, her heaviness, her long and sluggish days which I had encouraged despite knowing she found them aggravating. She complained constantly about the sticky weather, about wanting to go outside but not knowing where to go. When I suggested the beach, she said it was packed down there, that she couldn't take all the strangers and their stares. I too had noticed the way that people looked at Nim in public. She wasn't someone who kept a low profile, and that was especially true in the final months of her pregnancy. She'd taken to wearing crop tops, her bare belly hanging out, and eating ice pops that stained her lips blue. Nim was struggling to feel like herself, I could see that. She said she disliked being stared at, but I suspected that she was equally afraid of being ignored. She'd never been one to moan, to sit around all day, but now she acted as though trapped within her own body. Three weeks had passed since the day that she'd encouraged me, on the beach, to feel her belly for kicks, but it felt like years. Any quiet sense of wonder Nim had harboured at her changing form had by now evaporated entirely.

D'you want dinner? I asked.

Yeah, she said. Sure, whatever.

I scrambled some eggs and served them with bread and feta and tomatoes, and while we ate I sent out a couple of emails. Nim wolfed down her meal and then paced around the flat, huffing. She asked if I wanted to go for a walk, but when I said I had more work to finish she got frustrated and stormed out alone. She came back after twenty minutes, moisture dotting her upper lip, and slammed the door. I suggested she get an early night, and she scoffed.

That's one way to get rid of me, she said.

Her voice was vicious, and when I looked up her expression was even worse. She'd been stewing about something on her walk, that was obvious, and had come in with the intention of starting a fight. She was flushed with rage, her whole body tense. I'm not trying to get rid of you, I said.

Not yet. You need the baby out of me first.

I closed my laptop. Excuse me? I said.

All I am to you is fucking pregnant, Jules. Outside of this baby, I swear I don't exist at all. But what'll happen when I push it out? I'll be a husk, all used up. You won't want me anymore. Nobody will.

I shook my head, unbelieving. I was going to miss Nim desperately, surely she knew that. It was not only her who struggled to bring up what we would do after the labour. I was so filled with grief by the thought of her moving out that I found myself mostly unable to think about it, and yet whenever I realised this I felt guilty, because it meant in some way that I was dreading the arrival of the baby. Now, I stood up from my seat, and went to her. She had her arms crossed above her belly, her whole body so tense that touching her seemed impossible. She stared me out, scowling, as I stepped closer. In all of this, I'd never seen Nim cry properly. She did then, and with her tears came a slackness in her body, in which she allowed me to put my arms around her. Her firm belly pressed into my softer one. Her tears wet my neck.

I'm sorry, I said. I've been out a lot this week. I should have been here with you. It's not fair otherwise.

I don't know what's happening to me, she whispered. I don't feel like myself.

That night was the last before Gunk closed for summer. Nim was down for a shift and though I thought she seemed in need of rest, she insisted, like always, that she wanted to work. She raided my wardrobe and came out of the bedroom in a pink triangle bikini top that I hadn't seen for years and her old grey tracksuit bottoms, which were her only trousers that still fit. She was bigger than I'd ever seen, her belly shiny and dense, so full I swore I could see it pulsing. Her face was still puffy from crying, eyes a little swollen, but she seemed invigorated by the prospect of leaving the flat. I made myself a coffee and poured it over ice, and I walked to the club drinking it, Nim by my side. It made me feel light-hearted, vaguely kooky, to walk down the street supping from a china mug. Brighton was like that in the summer, full of character. On the Level, crusties bounced along a slackline, grubby kids fired at each other with water pistols and homeless couples spooned on the grass. If any of these people owned shoes, I couldn't see them. Sometimes the city felt devoid of life, of family. Other times, the place was bursting.

Nim and I got to the club after nine. She unloaded the dishwasher while I carried some crates of beer down the stairs to stack into the fridge. I brought the folding chair out from the back, so that Nim could sit down whenever she wanted. The DJ arrived, a man with a goatee who I'd known for years and yet barely spoken to, and started setting up. Nim offered him a beer, offered me one, then opened three. I hadn't seen her drink alcohol pregnant. For a moment I cringed, and then I caught myself. She was on some kind of quest that night, I understood, with her pink bikini top and her bottle of beer. She was trying to wrangle something of herself back, and I had no choice but to wish her luck with it.

Carlos took his place at the door, and slowly punters began to file inside. Nim doled out drinks, I punched digits into the card machine. The bass reverberated through my ankles. Sweat dripped from my armpits and soaked into the floor. I remembered the single summer, in the beginning of my marriage to Leon, when we had tried staying open after term ended and the students left the city. It had been a disaster, and by the end of the season we'd made a loss. Gunk was not the kind of venue that tourists sought out. We didn't serve fish-bowl cocktails, our DJs didn't take requests, and the dodgy staircase was not suited to stilettos. It had taken me years to navigate the chaos of running a venue, of working with Leon, and until Nim was hired nothing had ever felt entirely seamless. Now, my work had finally found its rhythm, just as everything was about to change. Leon was gone, and if he knew what was good for him, he wouldn't come back. Soon Nim would be gone too, and the bar would be manned by some lacklustre kid I'd only hired because they looked like Nim from a certain angle; had that same big mouth, that fuck-you spark in the eye. Carlos would remain on the door as long as we stayed open, veins popping out of his neck, biding his time before he could persuade me out on another date, another hook-up. Eventually I'd give in and marry him, secure a reliable father for the baby, please my parents.

Or perhaps tonight would be the end, would be all of it over. Perhaps Gunk would close for summer and never open again. I would stay home with the baby, Leon would sell up, Carlos would get a job elsewhere and Nim would dive into the life she was right now reaching out for, clad still in my bikini top: something to remember us by.

Nim drank four beers that night, sipping slowly as she worked. When she finished her final bottle, she dropped it into the big sack we used for recycling, and then she stepped out from behind the bar. I thought she was going to the toilet, but instead she walked into the middle of the dance floor with her arms in the air, bent at the elbows so that she was cradling her own head. She danced with her shoulders and hips, rocking her neck from side to side. The crowd of students parted for her, then formed a wide ring. Nim was like a repelling magnet, calm yet firm, creating space for herself, for her belly. When she turned in my direction I noticed that her eyes were closed, that she was smiling. The strobes above her elbows flashed and slid, catching the smoke from the machines in their glare. Nim continued to dance, the hair of her armpits showing, her head dipping as she swayed. I don't know how long I was watching before she opened her eyes and looked at me.

29

For a week, Nim and I barely left the flat. The slow-
ness came for me, finally, and I understood I could no
longer run. Together Nim and I ate and slept, ate and
slept. I felt pangs of jealousy towards her pregnancy,
quick and sharp, which surprised me. My old bitterness,
it turned out, had not retreated from me completely.
The fact was that I remained attached to my own useful-
ness, my capability, and now that I didn't have the club
to absorb me, nor Leon to make me feel in control, I
was envious of Nim, whose body maintained a constant
state of creation. In every minute, she was growing the
baby, feeding the baby, allowing them to live off her like

a parasite. In the beginning of our week at home, I'd hoped that, by mirroring Nim's physical existence, I might better make the baby mine. The reality was that I'd not acknowledged myself as a body for a long time, and doing so was a shock to me. Before Nim arrived in my life I hadn't exercised, I hadn't eaten properly. I'd allowed myself little sleep, even less touch. I'd been focused on chasing down things I couldn't hold: I'd craved status, admiration, control. Being around Nim, in the very end of her pregnancy, was different. It was tangible. Quite suddenly the physical world took over; it rose up and proved itself to be the more powerful. With this came a certain amount of letting go, a certain amount of surrender. I found I was ravenously hungry, that I could sleep for days.

In Nim's thirty-six-week midwife appointment, she was given four plastic syringes and advised to collect her early milk, called colostrum, and freeze it before labour. This was in case the baby had trouble feeding. Nim was not intending to feed, but she was intent on gathering colostrum, so that I could administer it in the early days of the baby's life. In the flat, Nim and I watched a YouTube video on how to hand express. I ran a bath, arranged the plastic syringes on a dinner plate, and boiled a jar for her to squeeze her milk into. It was evening. The YouTube video had advised that the space feel calm, so I lit three candles and arranged them around the bathroom. I'd crowded most of the plants in there, because I'd read online that they liked the humidity, and now the steam brought out a grassy smell from the soil. The mist was green. In the bath, Nim cupped her hand against her left breast and started to knead, just as we were shown in the video. We both watched her nipple closely, waiting. It was brown and dappled at the edges. After a minute or so, with no sign of milk, I suggested I leave her to it. I closed the bathroom door and sat on the sofa, tried to read one of the baby books I'd gathered from the charity shop.

I'd bought one book with a photograph on the cover of Earth painted onto a pregnant belly, the foetus done in green like a supercontinent. Inside, there was a printed photo of a real post-birth scene. There were no people in the image, only the mess that had been left behind. There was far more blood than I'd imagined, great pools of it. Something brown was smeared on the bed that I could only assume was shit. The placenta was a huge, black-red heart in a cardboard bowl. The book talked about something called ecstatic birth, claiming it was actually possible to orgasm during labour, since the hormone produced to stimulate contracting is the same as the hormone produced during sex. This was also true, one page stated, for breastfeeding. I liked flicking through this book, but it made me nervous. I knew that I could not contend with the viscerality, with the mayhem. It made my future with the baby seem clinical, propped up by sterilised bottles and zero shared genetics. The other book I'd bought was lilac, with mapped-out sleep schedules for every month of the baby's life. There was information in it that I recognised as outdated, like bolstering your baby's bottle with cereal to make them sleep longer. This comforted me, in a way. If the guidelines had been wrong for so many years, then perhaps whatever mistakes I was due to make would not be detrimental.

Ten minutes passed, maybe more. I resisted the urge to knock and ask Nim how it was going. Finally I got up for a glass of water and found myself standing with it, my ear pressed to the bathroom door. Nim? I called.

She didn't reply. I pushed the door gently, and she was there in the bath still, her breast in one hand, the jar in another. She didn't turn when I opened the door. It's not coming, she said.

I put my hand on her head. The video warned that it might take a few attempts, I said. I was at level with her face then. There's no pressure, I said. If it doesn't work, it doesn't work.

I went to the window and opened it, let the steam filter out. I asked her if she wanted me to try, and with her eyes closed, she nodded. I sat on the lip of the bath, rolled my sleeves up and put my hands into the water to warm them. Her left breast was more red than her right, and I was sure I could see bruises surfacing, the shape and size of thumb prints.

Have you tried both? I asked.

She nodded again. The right one less, she said.

I took the weight of her right breast in the palm of my hand. It felt different to mine, smaller and firmer. I kneaded the flesh a while, from underneath. Nim squeezed her eyes closed, exhaled a raggedy breath.

Tell me if hurts too much, I said. We can always try again tomorrow.

Nim did not respond, and I knew that she wouldn't tell me. I kept kneading, running over the YouTube video in my mind, simulating what I hoped was the rhythm of a pump. Nim didn't watch. I glanced up at her intermittently, to check her expression. Her bottom teeth were clamped onto her top lip, pushing the blood away beneath the skin, so a small area of white bloomed there. When no milk came, I shifted my hand a little closer to the nipple, so that my thumb and fingers were touching the edge of it when they squeezed. Nim was still holding the glass jar, one elbow leant on the edge of the bath, her legs bent up so her knees protruded from the water.

Nim, I whispered. Look.

On her nipple, four dots had emerged. They were the colour of custard, of pus. Breastmilk was both of those things, I supposed, or somewhere between the two. I continued to squeeze, as if stopping might make the dots disappear, and they each grew a little in diameter. Nim swept the jar underneath, caught the first drop as it fell. I continued to pump her breast, one more drop and then another. The amount was pitiful, really, not even a quarter of a teaspoon, yet Nim and I were euphoric. I moved over to the next breast, worked out a little more. In ten minutes, we had enough to fill one of the tiny syringes. Nim sucked the liquid up very slowly, and I carried it to the freezer on two upturned palms.

When I returned to the bathroom, Nim was lying back, mostly submerged, with her head on the lip of the bath. Her bare belly stuck up, blue veins growing across it like roots. I looked at her face, and couldn't tell if the drops there were tears or bathwater.

How do you feel? I asked. Is there any pain?

A bit, she said. She was looking at me intently, and her stare was made more intense by the wet shine of her eyes, her hair, her whole glistening body. Thank you, she said.

It's nothing, Nim.

She was watching me still. Not long now, she said.

I know. It hit me properly the other night, in the club.

D'you think we'll ever circle back? asked Nim. Her eyes were dreamy, somehow, out of focus.

To each other, you mean?

Who knows, she said. Maybe we'll end up together, somewhere down the line.

I laughed a bit. You think so?

She wasn't quite smiling, but almost. It's what other people do, isn't it? People with babies.

You don't care about what other people do, Nim.

She was smiling properly then, but she looked sad too, in the backs of her eyes. No, she said. I guess you're right.

30

I listened to her get out of the bath and then pad through into the bedroom, leaving wet footprints on the floor-boards that I would discover later. I listened to the water drain, to the plug let out a burp. I was on the sofa, not doing anything. I'd found myself spending time like that, since the club closed. Just sitting still, listening to Nim move about, not even scrolling my phone. I'd ground to a halt, while all around me time was whipping by. It was good, I thought, to be still before everything, to take stock. Nim came in wearing a big T-shirt and a pair of knickers, her belly making the cotton into a tent. She looked very clean, the ends of her nails bright white.

I've got to say it now, she said, or I never will.

I knew what was coming. All this time, I'd been waiting for it. I held my breath, tried very hard to let go, to pre-empt my own grief. Soon it would all be over, these last few months no more than a bubble that was always going to be popped, my life back to the same rhythms, the same bleak routines.

I'm in love with you, she said.

I stared at her. I attempted to pick up from her face some clue that this was a prank. Her words made no sense to me at all. My eyebrows drew together. She was stood still, in the middle of the room, and I rose from the sofa so that I was standing too.

You remember on the beach, said Nim. How I told you I had a crush on you when we first met?

I nodded, perplexed.

Well, it never went away. I hoped it would, but it hasn't. You used to ask me about her sometimes. The crush, I mean. The crush was you, Jules. It was so obvious to me that I couldn't believe you didn't see it.

I thought you were going to tell me you'd changed your mind, I said. About the baby.

Nim vibrated her lips, shook her head. Why d'you think I slept with Leon in the first place, Jules? I was trying to make you jealous. I wanted your attention.

Really? I said.

By the time I found out I was pregnant, said Nim, I was fully in love with you. It's ironic, I know, to be into someone because they clearly don't want any partner at all. But I figured that if I couldn't have you, at least the baby could.

I frowned. I thought she'd got things twisted. Even if she believed her own words, really she meant something else.

When I was so upset in my scan, she said, it was because pretending to be a couple tormented me. I keep finding myself dreaming of us being a fucking family, Jules. I'm delusional, just like my mother is. I know I am, but I can't stop.

I swallowed. I thought we'd got to the truth of it then, finally, to the meaning at the bottom of her words. Nim, I said. If you want to raise the baby, just say that. If you've changed your mind, tell me. You don't need to soften it by making stuff up, by trying to protect me.

Nim's face dropped. I thought she was going to cry, and in a way I wanted her to. I wanted to see some remorse breaking through, some pain. I didn't mind that she'd lied about being in love with me. I understood her reasons. I knew how hard it would be for her to admit that she no longer felt able to give her baby up. But now I'd worked it out, it made sense to talk it over properly, to come up with an arrangement. Maybe I could have the baby half the week, or maybe she could stay living here for a while after the birth. We had options, I wanted to tell her. She didn't have to spin stories.

Nim did not cry. Her sadness passed so fleetingly I wondered if I'd imagined it. She stepped towards me, and on her face was pure hate. I thought she was going to hit me. I sucked in a lungful of air. By then, her nose was close enough to mine that I could smell her breath, the tang of butter. When she spoke, it was in a whisper. There was a slight quiver on the edges of the words. Don't call me a liar, she said. My mum called me a liar, and look what happened then.

The whites of her eyes were pink, her mouth a hard line. She gave me the look only she could give, the look that made me wither, as if I were shrinking inwards from my own skin. I registered her words slowly, and as I registered them, I understood that they were a threat. If she'd not been trying to take the baby from me already, she would now. Regret crept over me. Like in a bad dream, I opened my mouth and no sound came. Nim turned. I heard her go into the bathroom to collect her trousers and shoes from the floor, and then she slammed the front door so hard that the whole flat shook, left a humming in my bones.

I felt quite sure that she would not come back, not ever. She would leave me just as she had left her mother. It made no sense – she was heavily pregnant, with nowhere to go – but Nim was not someone who made sense; she worked to her own logic, her own truth. I had been foolish enough to doubt that truth, and now she would punish me. I realised that, since Nim had told me about her past, I'd been waiting for her to disappear on me, just as she'd disappeared on her mother. Nim carried around with her a sense of foreboding, I'd always felt that, but learning of her history had made the agony she would cause me seem increasingly inevitable.

3 1

I was wrong about that, like I was wrong about most things. Nim returned to the flat an hour after she'd left. She didn't say a word to me when she got in, only gave me her same ruthless glare and slunk into the bedroom. I understood that she wasn't speaking to me, but that was OK for now, so long as she was there. Nim would not disappear on me for some hours more. She would do it when I least expected her to, as is her way.

Nim can be hotheaded and impulsive, but she can be wise, too. For someone so young, she's full of lessons. Perhaps if I hadn't been unwilling to learn, to listen, things would have been different. The truth was that after Leon, I didn't think of myself as a person who could be loved. I'd closed myself off to all that. The only person I'd imagined ever loving me again was a baby. Like most women, I'd been taught that romance and motherhood would be my reward. Since one of those had failed me, I'd put all my hopes into the other. For Nim, who'd been failed by her mother, it was the opposite way around. Sure, we should have been more imaginative; I see that quite clearly now. But it's never so easy, from the inside.

Nim woke me at two o'clock in the morning. I feel something, she said.

She was acting normal: no longer angry, not yet in pain. This was odd in itself, and I knew that it was happening. What kind of something? I asked.

I followed her into the living room, then left to make us each a cup of tea. When I went to her with it, she was twisted up on the sofa, squirming her legs and hooking her feet around her ankles. Make it cold, she said.

I filled a glass with ice and poured the tea over. I added a little honey; I thought the sugar would boost her energy. There were four weeks still until her due date. I didn't know if this was dangerous, and I didn't have the time to look it up. The moon was big in the window. I put a straw in the iced tea, so that Nim didn't have to sit upright in order to drink. She drained the whole glass. More, she said.

I filled the glass of ice this time with water; I didn't know if all that caffeine was a good idea. What's that? she spat, when I gave her the glass. I said I wanted more.

I apologised, brewed another tea. She sucked it down. Do you want anything to eat? I asked.

No way, she said. I feel sick.

I got out a saucepan in case she needed to throw up, and the moment I handed it to her she vomited all the tea straight back out again. It made a noise like a water slide, sloshing. The liquid looked exactly the same as it had two minutes before. I took it to the toilet, flushed it down. I was starting to panic then, just a little. I brought a cold flannel, and she lay back on the sofa with it over her forehead. She wiped her chin with the back of her hand. Her skin was damp, her pupils giant. In the lamplight she looked glossed.

Do you feel any contractions? I asked.

I don't know what I feel, she said.

I ran her another bath, and she got in. I lingered by the door, listening to her groans. She kept asking me to come in and wet her flannel under the cold tap in the sink. She was obsessed with cold things. I brought her a glass of ice cubes and she put one on her head. It sat upright on the shaved hair, slowly melting into her scalp. We were almost out of ice then. I refilled the tray, considered running to the shop, and realised it would be closed. I thought of waking up a neighbour, but decided to wait to see if Nim asked for more. Nobody had told me that she'd get obsessed with ice. Nobody had told me anything, I realised then.

After a couple of hours in the bath, Nim called me in and asked me to time her contractions. She'd been advised that they were supposed to last one minute each, with five minutes between, before she could go to the hospital. I timed four minutes between two contractions, then four and a half. Nim was too brave. I felt angry with her for that, worried it would get us in trouble.

Nim! I said. What the fuck? We have to go.

I called a taxi, hauled her out of the water and rubbed her down with a towel. Her body looked different: her nipples were so dark, the colour of soil, and her belly had dropped significantly lower. I helped her into clean clothes, stuffed some spares into a bag. In the lift, Nim didn't speak. She was shivering, breathing with her tongue stuck out her mouth, her eyes rolled back in her head. I wanted to apologise, but it seemed ridiculous to do it then.

She's not in labour, is she? the taxi driver asked through his window, when he pulled up.

No, I said.

Nim flared her nostrils, kept doing her spooky breathing. You're going to the hospital in the middle of the night, said the driver, but she's not in labour?

Fine, I said. She's in labour. So you're gonna leave her to give birth here on the street?

I don't want her giving birth in my car, either.

I can assure you that's not our plan, I said.

And if her waters break? There's a fine for that, you know.

If her waters break, we'll pay the fine. Jesus. Can we go, or do I have to call another cab?

The driver sighed, clicked a button to unlock the doors. Nim lay across the two back seats, and I got in the front. She'll need to wear her belt, said the driver.

I've not screamed at anyone, except for Leon, like I screamed at that taxi driver then. All the blood rushed to my face, and I shouted so loud that even Nim stopped her groaning. My eyes bulged and my neck bent unnaturally to the side. I must have looked possessed. I only shouted one word, but that word was enough: Drive.

So we drove, the moon framed in the windscreen, and no more words were exchanged. There were hardly any cars on the road. The lights of the city bled and squiggled in the windows. My eyes made spirals where spirals did not exist. I was tired, though not as tired as Nim, who breathed in the back seat like her insides were alight. When she went quiet, I put my hand through the gap in the seats and placed it on her elbow. Too hot, she said, flicking her arm to get me away.

I looked out and thought about how the next time we took this journey the baby would be here. I considered how it would feel to be shoved from a warm bloody cave, Nim's heart beating above like the sun, into this maze of pavements, of contradictory books on how best to hush your screams. What a hoodwink it was, to be born. Perhaps this explained why all my life I'd resented my parents. Maybe, I thought. But also I had stayed here, near them, in this city. I hadn't moved away for even a month, though I'd spent so many considering myself trapped. At some point I would have to ask why I'd chosen, every day of my grown life, to remain in Brighton. And when I asked myself this, the answer would surely be because I loved my parents, because I loved this stupid place. This was my home, dead for half the year and packed for the other, crawling with buskers and beggars and students. This was my home, and these were my people, too.

3 2

It was not dark in the hospital. It was not even night. Hospitals don't live by such rules. People go there to be born, or to die, or else to try to avoid dying. These people are led by their bodies, are living outside of time. The waiting area was very bright, bustling. Nim and I stood around waiting. After I gave Nim's name, there was another wait. How long for, I couldn't say. It was the waiting area, after all. Like few things, it gave us what it promised. Nim put her forehead to the wall and swayed back and forth, rolling her head against the paint. Her groans had become long and deep, like a dog growling. Finally someone brought us out a wheelchair, and I pushed her through into the ward.

Run, she demanded.

I didn't know if she was joking, but I did as I was told.

In the ward she had her blood pressure taken and was given a vaginal examination. She hated that. There were tears on her face. She still had her same dark-eyed look, the circumference of her pupils wide enough to pull in the entire hospital, the entire universe. It was as if her eyes were trying to pull the baby out, through sheer pressure. But the baby was the one thing her pupils couldn't find, or couldn't fathom. I fed Nim sips of water from a plastic cup. She kept asking for ice, but I had none. There was a blue curtain pulled around us. The maternity ward was full of screams, of sobs, of guttural objection. Every pitch available was being hit by someone. I paid for a coffee and black sludge pulsed from the machine, far too hot to drink.

When I returned, we were told that Nim was in the right stage of labour to be allowed her own room, but there were no rooms available, and there were no pools either. I wanted to ask how long, but the midwife was already gone. Nim was crying. Fuck, she called, making the word go on. She called it out lots of times, from the base of her throat.

I put my hands on her face, but they were hot from holding the coffee cup, and I took them away. You're doing so good, I said. I would have liked to say something profound, at least original, but I wasn't capable of putting the words together.

Finally we were given a room, with no pool. Nim was brought some gas and air, and she really went in on it. Her growls became a hissing. I realised the seriousness of her pain, seeing how thirstily she sucked, and when she wasn't sucking she clasped the tube like it was the only thing keeping her alive. The room hushed around her hissing noises, then her long breaths out. We had a big window, just as when I'd visited Leon here, and in it the sun was coming up over the city. Cars began to cruise the veiny roads. The sun was an organ, bleeding out into the sky. The continuity of everything seemed almost rude to me, then. How dare a new day arrive, when the baby was not yet born?

The hissing and the sunrise made me realise how long we'd been going. Seven hours, eight. I wanted to reach through into the future and pluck the baby out. I wanted to hold them, and for the holding to be right now.

I drank another coffee, and when I came back Nim was having another examination. She wasn't progressing, they said. She hadn't progressed in three hours. I asked why. I wanted answers, but there were none. When would this get beautiful? I wanted to know. Nim kept hissing. She was on all fours on the hospital bed, wearing her paper gown, so that the midwife could measure how dilated she was. She had another contraction, and when it came she pushed herself back onto her haunches and stuck her naked arse in the air, so I could see the purple folds of her vulva, the hot pink inside. The hissing was so intense then, it filled my ears and ricocheted. I stepped to the top end of the bed and studied Nim's damp face. She looked defeated.

What do you need? I asked.

I thought she might ask for more drugs, for an emergency caesarean, and with me that would have been fine, that would have made perfect sense, but she didn't. Touch me, she said. Her voice was off-key from the drugs, there was too much air in it. It was as if we were speaking across ozone. I put my hands on her shoulders, and massaged. More, she moaned. More.

I moved my hands lower, and she seemed to prefer that. I massaged her lower back, and she gyrated her hips in the air. I was stood behind her, and I began to circle my hips with her own. She was bare against my jeans, and there were two or three other people in the room, looking on. She didn't appear to feel shame. Wherever she was, shame did not exist. Nim's entire sense of self had evaporated from her, and was now the condensation dripping from the big windows. Nim was a splitting body, a raw soul. She arched her back, tipped her head to the ceiling and roared. I hadn't heard such noise come from her in hours, maybe in forever. I stepped back from her, and as I did so I found that I was soaked all down my crotch, I was wet with her waters, and they were still coming. The puddle grew on the floor, catching the sun, which had risen fully now and was white-yellow in the pink sky. The sunlight gave Nim's waters the look of a mirror. In it I saw the gridded hospital ceiling, the peach light.

A midwife rushed through with towels. There was renewed energy in the room. Things were moving again. We were getting closer. After Nim's waters broke, she progressed very quickly. Within half an hour she was dilated enough to start pushing. She hadn't changed position on the hospital bed, and while she pushed I stood bent low, my face very close to hers, and I whispered to her, about how well she was doing, about how soon it would be over. The midwife announced that she could see the baby's head and I stepped down to look at his damp, wrinkled scalp, the fine hair soaked with blood, streaked with a white paste that I cannot now resist describing as gunk, and then I returned to Nim's face and I kissed her salty forehead. I was crying and she was crying and nothing mattered then apart from the baby's safe arrival. In that sense it was the plainest moment I've ever experienced in my life.

When he came he was a blue squirm, soaking wet, the umbilical cord a long, plasticky rope. He opened his mouth and screamed that he was alive. The midwife placed him on Nim and he turned his scrunched-up face into her skin and right then the two of them looked so separate, to me, and that separateness was miraculous and tragic at once. I looked at Nim, her face soaked with sweat and tears, and I wanted to tell her that she and the baby were everything, that they were the yolk at the centre of my life, that I had been wrong in a thousand ways. But Nim was not finished yet. She was told by the midwife that she had to pass the placenta, after which she would be checked for tears. The baby was given to me. To facilitate skin-to-skin I quickly removed my T-shirt and, since I'd forgotten to put on a bra when we left the flat, I stood there with my breasts out, not caring, holding his damp little body against mine. His first breaths moved through him in shudders. His eyes were closed, and I laughed that he appeared to have gone back to sleep at his own party, as if being born meant so little to him. In my arms he was a light source, an impossible beam, a strobe cutting through the dance floor. He was so bright that looking at him hurt my eyes. I could not look away.

33

The baby is four days old and I am yet to sleep for longer than two hours at a time. All I've eaten since he was born is cereal. We go to the supermarket, pick up Weetabix for dinner and Coco Pops for dessert. The shop is bright and garish; I walk around the place squinting, the baby in his sling. In a futile grapple for nutrients, I buy milk made from pea protein. I walk home with the bag slung over my shoulder, cradling the baby's feet loosely in my cupped hands. In the flat, I remove him from the sling and shimmy him into the bouncer. I sit over him, rocking his chair with one foot, to eat my cereal. His cheeks jog. He watches me. I wipe pea milk from my chin. He blinks. I wonder if, with that blink, he's trying to tell me that he loves me. His eyes glaze over, and he falls asleep. I keep bouncing, knowing better by now than to stop.

Something changed in me, when I watched the baby get born. I realised it was not in fact possible to close myself off to love. I realised that self-reliance, this plan I had to require nothing and no one, was no more than a fiction. I realised that I could not be a mother in a vacuum; I could not be anyone much. The fact of it is that people come from each other. We need each other in order to live. I didn't have to give birth myself in order to realise this. I only had to witness a birth.

Under my thigh, my phone vibrates. I pick it up, and Nim's name is on the screen. I answer, and am crying before I manage to speak. Hello? I say. The word catches in my throat, and I cough to clear it. Hello? I say again.

Her voice sounds far away. Jules, she says.

Are you safe?

Yes.

Where are you?

I'm at Leon's.

At Leon's?

I took your key from the flat, when I first realised I was in labour. I thought it would be the right place to come.

She went to Leon's. It makes perfect sense. I don't know why I haven't considered it before. Leon's away at rehab, his place standing empty. I imagine her now on his big leather sofa, the slight linger of bleach in the air from all my cleaning, a maternity pad bulging in her knickers.

How's the baby? asks Nim.

He's good. He's here.

I'm sorry I scared you.

Well, I'm sorry I accused you of lying.

I wasn't trying to punish you, Jules. Or not completely. I was trying to punish myself, I think.

Why would you do that?

Because I did exactly what my mother does, without even realising.

In what way?

I fell in love with the idea of you, and I lost myself in pursuit of it.

What idea was that?

That you'd take care of me.

But you need taking care of, Nim. Everybody does.

You don't, she says.

I'm so pleased by that glimmer of defiance that I let myself smile. I've missed her spirit. Of course I do, I say. I've been wrong, alright? I don't know what this is between us, but I think I might need it. I think I might need you.

She's silent for a moment. In the speaker of the phone, I listen to her breathing. What are we going to do? she says.

Would you consider coming back here, staying for a while?

I wait for her answer, my heart beating in my wrists. Maybe, she says. But I don't want to be his mother, Jules. I'm sure of that. I'm not ready. I might never be.

That's OK, I say. You can live here and not be his mother. *I'm* his mother, in fact.

It's only as I say these last words that I realise they're true. Since I answered the phone, my foot has not stopped bouncing the chair. In it, the baby snores. It feels strange, maybe anticlimactic, to finally give myself the word. Mother. I've yearned for it for so long, but when it comes, I'm surprised to find how little it matters. What matters is the baby, here with me.

For Nim and me, there is no word either, no neat category. We're more than friends, less than lovers. We're intimate but not sexual. I'm old enough to be her young mother, young enough to be her older girlfriend. We've slept with the same man, worked the same job. We lived as housemates but we shared a bed. Now, she's had a baby but the baby is mine. It occurs to me that perhaps this has been the problem, for Nim and me. We've been caught up in trying to define what we have. I tried to limit her to employee, to housemate, to surrogate. In turn, her approach was expansion; she reached up for romantic love. I see that we've been trapped by language, by legitimacy. But there is no need.

Nim agrees to come over. She doesn't say how long she will stay. An hour, a night, a year. I order her a taxi through an app on my phone. I don't know how well she's recovered from the birth, how far she feels able to walk. She arrives twenty minutes later. In that time, the baby has woken up, cried, been fed. He's alert now, more so than I've seen him yet. It's as if he knows she's coming. I leave him on the playmat while I answer the door. He stares at the ceiling with purpose. In the doorway, Nim looks different. She's no longer pregnant, a fact I had forgotten. She's wearing Leon's clothes: his beat-up leather jacket, the T-shirt with the squiggly graphic that he was wearing the night I met him. I didn't know he still had that, and it feels both obvious and unbelievable that she has chosen to put it on, the perfect fluke. Nim looks down at the graphic, because I am.

If I knew my outfit would get so much attention, she says, I would have tried a bit harder.

I laugh. I pull her into a hug. I hold her too tight, for too long a time. Her neck smells like soap, her clothes like must. I want to breathe her in and breathe her in. After we break apart I go to apologise, for grabbing hold of her and not letting go, but when I open my mouth to speak she takes my hand between the two of hers, and she holds it, watching me. The last time I looked into her face like this, properly, was the moment the baby came. We were both crying then, and we are both crying now.

Can I see him? she whispers.

I peer at her, trying to gauge how she really feels about the baby. I wonder if she's scared to see him, if she's hopeful, if by asking she's only being polite. I wonder if I will ever get better at reading her. I nod and turn down the hall, walk towards the living room, Nim following behind. We move through the corridor. I don't know if we are walking slowly or if it only feels slow. I have a bizarre vision in which the walls and the floor are the wet, crimson edges of a great birth canal, Nim and I being swept through. The shutters are open in the living room, the light flooding in, so that as we get closer to the doorway, the brightness lifts and lifts. I can hear the baby making his tiny newborn noises, his snuffles and creaks. In a matter of seconds, the three of us will be together. What will happen next, I cannot say. There's no format for this, so we have no choice but to make it up. For now, the brightness pulls us deeper, pulls us in, and floods.

ACKNOWLEDGEMENTS

Thank you to everyone who read *Send Nudes* and liked it, who bought a copy or borrowed one or recommended it to a new reader. Thank you to Niki Chang, perfect collaborator and friend and everything I could have wished for in an agent. Thank you to Allegra Le Fanu, my editor, for your feedback and support and unwavering trust through these last manic years of having babies and writing books. Thank you to Angelique Tran Van Sang, who offered me the book deal that started it all. Thank you to Brittani Davies, my publicist, and Saba Ahmed, my copyeditor, and Lauren Whybrow and everyone else at Bloomsbury, for holding *Gunk* and for helping to set it free. Thank you to Sheena Patel, for a conversation in emails which lit up what I'd been trying to do with this novel. Thank you to Alix Eve, for setting the timer in Rich Mix all through our bleak winter spent writing together. Thank you to Alice Zoo, early reader and generous friend, for your thoughts on the first draft I ever felt willing to share. Thank you to Alexis Ward, for pointing out the gunk a new baby comes out covered in. Thank you to Jelly and Bren, my guardian angels, for living inspiring lives. Thank you to every member of my insane and loyal family. Thank you to Jacob, for being the kindest person I've ever met, and finally thank you to the kids, who make it hard, but who also make it possible.

ABOUT THE AUTHOR

SABA SAMS was raised in Brighton and now lives in London. She was selected for *Granta*'s Best of Young British Novelists in 2023. Her short story collection *Send Nudes* was awarded the Edge Hill Short Story Prize 2022 and was shortlisted for the University of Swansea International Dylan Thomas Prize 2023. The story 'Blue 4eva' from the collection was awarded the BBC National Short Story Award. *Send Nudes* was selected as a book of the year by the *Guardian*, *Stylist*, *Vogue*, *Glamour*, *Cosmopolitan*, *Evening Standard*, *Irish Independent*, *AnOther*, Foyles and bookshop.org, and was named a *Sunday Times* paperback of the year in 2023.

A NOTE ON THE TYPE

The text of this book is set in Perpetua. This typeface is an adaptation of a style of letter that had been popularised for monumental work in stone by Eric Gill. Large scale drawings by Gill were given to Charles Malin, a Parisian punch-cutter, and his hand-cut punches were the basis for the font issued by Monotype. First used in a private translation called 'The Passion of Perpetua and Felicity', the italic was originally called Felicity.